D1458008

ANGEL
IN
DISGUISE

ANGEL
IN
DISGUISE

•

KRISTIN
HUNGENBERG

AVALON BOOKS
THOMAS BOUREGY AND COMPANY, INC.
401 LAFAYETTE STREET
NEW YORK, NEW YORK 10003

ABP- 4392

PRINTED IN THE UNITED STATES OF AMERICA
ON ACID-FREE PAPER
BY HADDON CRAFTSMEN, SCRANTON, PENNSYLVANIA

This book is dedicated to my husband, Dave
And to my Dad.

Chapter One

"U h-oh," Sydney muttered to herself as she glanced up at the sky. "Where did that come from?" Her horse's ears pricked back toward her at the sound of her voice. "Jared's going to skin my hide, Blaze." With a light lift of her hand and a touch from her left heel, Blaze spun around and headed for home.

The easy responsiveness of her horse brought a smile to her lips. He was the smartest horse she had ever trained and a dream to ride. He was her pride and joy and made training her other horses much easier. She used Blaze in a number of different ways while training her young horses to work under saddle, but even so, her brother Jared had been livid when she had turned down a hefty

1

sum of money offered for Blaze. She had told Jared that Blaze saved her all kinds of time in her training, but he knew that she had kept him because she couldn't bear to part with him. Jared thought she was too soft to train horses for a living. He wrongly assumed that she'd keep every horse she had. Even though she'd like to, she knew Blaze was the only horse she could keep for herself. She couldn't afford to make any more exceptions.

It was so easy to lose track of time when riding Blaze that she hadn't noticed the dark gathering of clouds that had sunk out of the sky to envelop her in a mist of gray. The wind had picked up and tiny snowflakes had already begun to drift lazily toward the ground. She knew the forecast called for at least six inches of snow by nightfall, but she had expected to be back long before the storm hit.

She glanced down at her watch and pulled it closer to her eyes to check again. The day was almost over, and somewhere along the way she had lost two whole hours. She couldn't believe it. And she was a good seven miles from home to boot. Blaze picked up on the tension coursing through her and automatically broke into an easy lope. The snowflakes were beginning to get heavier and fatter, and the icy wind picked up intensity and whipped them around her face.

At least she had one thing going for her—the

ground was even and smooth. With a small nudge of her heel, Blaze picked up his speed, and she concentrated on watching the fence line. Luckily she had worked her way out to the outer boundaries of the ranch and was riding not too far from the highway. She could follow the fence back to the lane that wound between the gently curving hills, and from there it would be easy enough to travel the four miles back to the house.

The weather could change so rapidly in the foothills of Colorado that it was always a good idea to pay attention to the sky. Jared was going to kill her when he found out she had been playing with her horse without a thought for the weather. At least she wouldn't have to hear about it right away. Jared was in Arizona visiting their parents, and she had the house to herself. Maybe she wouldn't even have to tell him about this episode. What he didn't know couldn't hurt him—or more important, her.

A loud pop brought her out of her thoughts, and she instinctively lifted the reins. Blaze slowed down and pricked his ears forward as Sydney looked around. It had sounded like a gunshot. The land on both sides of the highway was private property and hunters weren't allowed. Another blast sounded off to her left. There was a small rise between the fence and the highway, so she couldn't see what was going on, but she knew it had to be coming from the road. Why would someone be shooting a gun by the road?

A distress signal was three gunshots in quick succession, but no one would need that on a well-traveled highway. Traffic wasn't that thick between Fort Collins and Laramie, but enough cars and trucks came along to be of help if someone needed it. This didn't make sense.

Another shot made her jump as the loud report sounded closer than before. She and Blaze weren't far from the lane to her house now, and she urged him forward at greater speed as anxiety began to curdle in her stomach. The wind was beginning to howl, and she knew those shots had to be close for her to hear them so well over the storm.

A cattle guard in the lane was the only opening in the fence, but she didn't even slow down as she turned Blaze toward it and effortlessly jumped across. In three long strides Blaze topped the rise, and she pulled back sharply on the reins as the highway came into view. Blaze stopped on a dime as her mouth dropped opened at the scene taking place before her.

A police car was blocking the gravel road that was the only entrance to her family's property. The blue and red lights were still flashing, but it was obvious the police officer was no longer in control. One man was lying on the ground, and the officer was frantically struggling with another man. The fight was consuming his entire attention, and from the energy he was expending it was obvious it was a life-or-death situation. Sydney couldn't actually see a weapon, but she instinctively knew that the man had a knife. Before she could make a sound, a third young man with a gun in his hand swung at the back of the police officer's head. The officer's knees folded under him, and he sank listlessly to the ground. The man with the gun fumbled for a moment with something around the officer's waist and stood up with the policeman's gun belt. The man let out a piercing war whoop as he swung the belt around his head, before kicking the officer in the back, sending him rolling down the incline beside the lane.

Sydney didn't know what to do as she watched two of them have a conversation before the one with the gun gave another screeching yell, firing the gun into the air. He ran around and jumped into the police car while the other one helped the man on the ground into the silver Mercedes that was parked in front of the Colorado State Patrol car. With a screech of burning rubber they gunned their engines and sped off down the highway.

The whoosh of the wind in her ears was the only sound as she stared at the highway in a daze. Blaze shifted under her and Sydney closed her mouth with a snap. Those men had just brutally attacked an officer! With a sick feeling in her stomach she remembered the three gunshots she had already heard. The one man on the ground had limped to the car—he might have taken one shot, but what about the other two?

"Oh man," Sydney muttered out loud as she swallowed convulsively. The urge to throw up was strong, but she held it down as she nudged Blaze forward. She was almost afraid to look. Blaze slid down the slope, the snow making the grass beside the highway slippery. The officer hadn't moved. Sydney stepped down from the saddle and held on to Blaze for a moment as she caught her balance. Her knees were wobbling and her teeth were chattering, but it wasn't from the cold.

She had taken a first aid class in high school years ago, and she tried to remember what to do first. She pulled frantically at her riding glove until it ripped off and gently felt along his neck for a pulse. He was lying facedown in the snow, but she was afraid to move him. A steady beat pulsed against her fingers as she finally found the groove along his windpipe.

"Okay, now what? You're supposed to call 911, but I need a phone." Shock at witnessing such violence was slowing her thought processes, and she shook her head as she tried to think. Wait a minute. She was right by a highway. Surely a passing motorist would have a cellular phone. She stood up and looked up and down the road, straining her ears to hear over the wind, but there was nothing.

"Great. . . . Okay, okay, get a grip!" Hearing her own voice calmed her somewhat, and she looked back down. She remembered that he'd been on his feet until he'd been hit with the butt of the gun. After the push in his back, he'd rolled sideways rather than head over heels. Chances were he hadn't broken his neck. She didn't have a choice; she had to move him to see if he was breathing.

Gently she pulled on his shoulder and rolled him onto his side. Blood was trickling down the side of his face. She traced it back to a small cut over his eye and breathed easier. It was a lot of blood, but the cut didn't look that serious. His eye was swelling shut, and he had a huge knot on his cheekbone, but she didn't see any bullet holes. Her fingers were shaking as she held them under his nose, but the warm trickle of air against her skin was obvious. He was breathing.

She slid her hands under his heavy jacket feeling for blood, but there wasn't any. She stood up and checked his legs as well. His tan pants were soaking wet, but it was all from the snow, not from any wounds. His dark eyelashes contrasted with the pallor of his skin, and she frantically tried to recall what to do for a concussion. That he needed more medical attention than she could provide was the only thing she knew for certain.

Glancing up to the highway again in hope of getting someone else to help gave her another shock. She could barely see the road. Snow was falling so thickly now that visibility was down to ten feet at the most. The slope of the incline was blocking most of the wind, but the bite of the air hit her in a wave as she realized that her fingers were already numb. Her boots and jeans were drenched from standing in the snow that had accumulated in the grassy area beside the road.

If she was cold, he had to be freezing. Most of his clothing was saturated, and he wasn't wearing gloves or a hat. She at least had a black, floppy-brimmed hat covering her hair, keeping most of it dry. His dark hair was matted with snow and blood, and she knew hypothermia was going to be his next problem.

There still wasn't a sound or sight of a vehicle in either direction. ''Couldn't those guys at least have left his car?'' she asked as she looked up at the sky. They'd just left him out here to freeze to death. Maybe they hadn't shot him, but they might as well have. If she hadn't seen it happen she wouldn't have known there was a body beside the road. Nausea whipped through her system, and she bent over to take a deep breath.

''Okay . . . okay. I can do this,'' she said as she swallowed hard. ''I'm going to have to get him back to the ranch.'' It was snowing too hard to wait any longer for help. As it was she'd be lucky to make it back to the house. Snow was piling up at an alarming rate, and it wouldn't take long before the lane back to the house would be indistinguishable from the rest of the land.

Carefully she walked around and bent over to grasp the officer under the arms. Her feet slipped in the wet grass, but she dug in her heels until she managed to pull him halfway up the slope. Blaze was still standing calmly with his tail tucked against the wind, and she patted his neck as she pulled him forward until the saddle was even with the officer's feet.

She walked back and easily pushed the officer to a sitting position. She squatted down and got her weight under her as she pulled with everything she had and lifted him up. She let his weight carry them forward and leaned him up against Blaze's side. The horse shifted against the unexpected weight, but he didn't move away.

"Good boy, Blaze. Good boy." Sydney took a moment to catch her breath as she flopped the officer's arms over the saddle. She dropped down, put her shoulder under his hips and heaved. When she reached her full height his body was mostly over the horse, and she finished the job by shoving him the rest of the way with her hands.

Years of riding had developed the muscles in her legs way beyond the strength of a normal woman her height. At five feet seven inches, she was a little taller than the average woman and twice as strong. Her legs and arms were hard and firm, and there wasn't a spare ounce of fat on her trim physique. Carrying heavy water buckets and large hay bales had a lot to do with it as well. She was suddenly doubly thankful for her strength because without it she wouldn't have been much use to the policeman.

Panting from the exertion, she looked around for her glove but didn't see it. The snow was so thick now she could barely make out the head of her horse, and she stayed next to him as she moved to his head and grasped the reins. She led him up the incline and pointed him down the lane. Luckily the reins on his bridle were long, and she stretched them over the officer's back as she mounted behind the saddle.

This was the first time she had ever ridden double on Blaze. He didn't seem to mind the extra weight, ducking his head against the savage wind as he moved off toward home. There was a gate in the fence next to the cattle guard, and Sydney slid off to open it.

The snow was already beginning to drift against the posts, and she had to tug to slip the barbed wire over the post before she could drag the gate free. Blaze had turned his tail to the wind while he was waiting, and she marveled again at what a wonderful horse he was. She knew that if she had been riding any other horse, she and the officer wouldn't stand much of a chance in making it back. None of her other horses were trained well enough to stand and wait the way Blaze was.

Once she led him through she took a moment to pat his sleek black coat before mounting behind the saddle again. Blaze was as dark as tar with only one marking—a white lightning bolt down the center of his face. Blaze wasn't a very original name but it certainly fit him.

Time was running out on them, and she didn't bother to close the gate as she urged Blaze into the wind. The snow was blowing so hard around them that Sydney lost all sense of direction. She couldn't see far enough to tell if they were even on the lane. Blaze was still moving confidently forward, and Sydney realized she was going to have to trust his judgement. They could be going around in circles for all she knew, but instinctively she trusted her horse. He was their only hope.

The skin on her face and ears burned with an icy fire, and she tucked her chin into her sheepskin-lined denim jacket. She held the reins with her gloved hand and buried her naked hand in her coat pocket. Even so, her body was beginning to feel like a huge block of ice, and she shuddered to think how cold the officer must be by now. Her faded blue jeans had turned a dark navy from the wet, and they blended now with the deep blue of the officer's jacket.

Snow was sticking to her eyelashes, making it impossible for her to open them more than a crack. Her world had narrowed to the policeman's back in front of her as she tried not to think about how far they had yet to go.

Something seemed different and Sydney struggled to figure out what it was. She opened her eyes a little farther and managed to look up. Blaze was standing with his head down, and he was no longer moving. That was it—they were stopped. Her heart lurched painfully until she realized there was something in front of Blaze's head. Pulling her chin out of the collar of her jacket, she looked up higher. That something was the pillar to the front steps of her two-story ranch home. Holy cow! Blaze had done it.

There was no time to lose, but moving was difficult. Pain sliced along her nerves, shooting up into her back as she slid to the ground. She ignored it and reached up to pull the officer down. Most of her energy was gone, and when his body slid down on top of her, he knocked her flat.

Panting now from the strain, she struggled out from under him and slid her hands under his arms. She had to sit down on the steps and push with her heels to bring him up the two steps to the front porch. Snow had piled high along the wooden planks to the front door, and it made it easier to slide him along until she opened the door and dragged him in.

The release from the wind knocked her down, and she lay there for a moment to catch her breath. The icy wind was curling around the front door and blowing snow over the policeman's black boots, which were still dangling over the threshold. She knew Blaze was trustingly waiting for her out by the steps, and it gave her renewed energy as she picked herself off the floor.

She dragged the officer a little farther into the foyer and closed the door on the storm. She flicked on a light and looked down at the man. Snow was caked around his nose and mouth, and she frantically dropped to her knees to wipe it away. She felt for his pulse and drooped from relief when she still felt it beating steadily against her frozen fingertips.

It was going to take a lot of effort to do anything for the officer, and she couldn't afford to leave her horse unattended that long. Blaze would have to come first. The heater was blowing along the floor; she could feel the warm air against the stiffness of her jeans. That at least would be a start on warming him up until she got back from the barn.

Jared's lariat hung beside the door underneath his jacket, and Sydney grabbed it as she opened the door and braced herself against the onslaught of the wind. She looped one end around the front pillar and held onto the other end as she grabbed Blaze's reins and headed for the barn.

The barn had been built in the early 1900s and the huge red doors were only about twenty yards from the house. The pens and pastures spread out behind the barn on the far side. The rope was long enough to make it that far, and she wrapped it around one of the U-shaped bars attached to the doors. She had to slam her hand against the board that rested in the bottom of the U-shaped bars to free it and open the door.

The wind whipped one door out of her hand to bang against the wall. She ignored it and led Blaze inside. Her fingers were so numb, she had a terrible time uncinching her saddle, but finally she managed to pry the leather loose. She dumped her saddle on the floor and led Blaze into the nearest stall. She left him only long enough to grab a scoop of grain and his horse blanket from the tack room. Heated water flowed into tanks in each stall, and she was glad she had spent the money on heating two years ago.

Blaze was happy to munch on his grain as she slid his blanket over his back and buckled it on. She grabbed an armful of hay and filled his hay net before closing the wooden stall door and heading back. She didn't have time to do any more for him and trusted that his own body heat would warm him up under his blanket.

The end of the lariat was still hanging from one of the doors, and she hung on to it for dear life as she blocked the barn doors shut and struggled back through the snow. She left the rope on the front porch and stumbled for the door. Her hands were too numb to hang onto the door, and it whipped out of her hand and slammed back against the wall with a loud crash. She had to use her body to push it closed and fumbled for a second before she finally got it to latch. Slumping against the wall, she waited a moment to catch her breath yet again.

Chapter Two

A scraping noise on the floor startled her and she turned around. The police officer was conscious, his one good eye open and his hands fumbling clumsily at his waist. Sydney wasn't sure what he was doing at first, and then it dawned on her.

She put her hands up over her head. "I think they took your gun."

The officer's hands stilled and he looked up.

"At least one of them was firing a handgun. I'm assuming it was yours. They took your car and left you beside the road." Holding her hands up took too much effort, and she let them drop. "You're lucky to be alive—that storm almost killed us both."

The officer opened his mouth and tried to speak, but nothing came out. He tried again and his voice came out in a croak. "Who are you?"

"Sydney Carrigan. You might have noticed the Carrigan Ranch sign hanging over the lane out there by the road. I brought you back to the house." She stopped speaking as she noticed how hard he was shivering. He was doing his best to hold his head up to watch her, but she knew he couldn't manage it for long.

"If you're going to live through this, we need to do something . . ." Her voice trailed off as the lights went out. She heard him gasp before loud scraping noises started against the floor. He was backing away from her! He must think he'd been kidnapped or something.

She put out her hands to placate him even though he couldn't see her. "Wait! Wait . . . listen, I'm not one of the bad guys. I'm trying to help. Really." The scraping noises stopped. "You maybe don't remember that it was snowing when you stopped that car out there, but now it's turned into a raging blizzard. The storm put the power out. Listen to the wind."

It was eerie listening to the cry of the wind in the pitch-dark. Sydney shivered. "I'll just go get a flashlight, okay? I'm not going to hurt you. Just stay there a minute."

He didn't answer as she moved off to her right.

There was a closet not far from the front door where they kept their heavy outerwear, small tools, and a couple of flashlights. She slid her hand along the closet door until she found the doorknob. Once inside she had to feel along the top shelf and knocked down a couple of cans. She jumped at the racket they made hitting the floor. ''Just knocked a can over,'' she said to reassure him. She brushed over a hammer and a pair of pliers before her hand finally settled on a flashlight.

She turned it on and swept it over the floor toward him. He closed his eye against the glare and she quickly turned it away and put it on herself. ''Sorry, didn't mean to blind you.'' She kept the light on the floor in front of her as she moved closer to him. ''Okay, listen—this is the way it is. We're both soaking wet, and there's no longer any heat in this house. There are fireplaces though.'' She stopped talking to think and made a snap decision. ''There's a bedroom just down this hall. Do you think you can make it that far?''

He turned his head to look, and she turned the flashlight that way so he could see the twenty feet of shiny floorboards between them and Jared's room. His teeth were chattering so loud now, she could hear them over the wind. She sucked in her breath at the thought of what she had to do now. ''Those wet clothes are going to have to come off first.''

His eye snapped back to her face.

"I'm sorry." Suddenly the frustration of dealing with such an awkward situation made her angry. "It's not like I'm going to attack you, you know. If I wanted you dead, I wouldn't have bothered to throw you over my horse and waste all that time moving so slowly for the four miles back here." Her anger drained away when he just continued to look at her. It occurred to her that he wasn't as lucid as she thought he was. "Look, you're not going to warm up as long as you're wet. You want to be warm again, don't you?"

He moved his head enough that she took it for a nod. His hands moved for the zipper on his jacket, but he didn't have the coordination to grasp it. Her own fingers weren't much better, but with his help she managed to wrestle him out of his clothes. He didn't say a word, and she tried to ignore the fact that she was undressing a man. Hardly the way she would have pictured doing that for the first time in her life.

When he was stripped to a pair of dark blue boxer shorts, she grasped his arm and helped him up to his feet. That he wasn't the type for tight-fitting underwear certainly helped matters in her opinion. Especially since he had a wonderful body. She had seen her brothers in various stages of undress off and on throughout her life, but nothing had prepared her for the shock of seeing so much skin on this man.

His skin was smooth and almost hairless, with just a few dark hairs in the center of his chest. It was obvious that he worked out. Muscles rippled under his tight skin and his belly was flat and hard. She had a picture in her mind of cops eating doughnuts and going to flab, but he blew that scenario to bits.

He was still shivering uncontrollably, and his balance was way off, but she managed to half carry him, half guide him down the hall to Jared's room. Her legs were burning from the strain of holding him up by the time they reached Jared's bed. She eased him down, and he immediately sprawled back, too weak to sit up by himself. She pulled the covers back, helped him roll under them, and tucked them up around him. Sinking down beside him, she wiped her shaky hand across her forehead, tipping her hat back.

The pain in her own hands and feet goaded her to stand again, and she hurried over to the fireplace and grabbed some of the wood stacked beside it. The fire took twice as long as normal to start, but eventually she managed it. The orangish yellow flame brightened the room and traced dancing shadows along the wall. The heat was unmistakable, but she didn't have time to enjoy it yet.

"I'll be right back," she said as she turned to look at him. The covers were rippling from his shivering, but his eyes were closed and he didn't respond. Using the flashlight, she found several comforters in a hall closet and brought them back to drape over him. Heading out again, she went down to the basement and grabbed two kerosene lanterns her family used when they went fishing. She lighted one in the bathroom and the other she set beside the bed.

She was going to have to clean him up and do something about that cut over his eye, but first she needed to warm up. With the help of the flashlight she made it upstairs to her own room. She pulled out her thickest pair of sweats and two sweatshirts, as well as her thick wool socks and a pair of slippers. Getting her own clothes off was almost harder than removing his had been. Her fingers were warming up now and using them was extremely painful. She threw her wet clothes in a pile in her own bathroom and quickly pulled on her soft snuggly sweats.

Her dry clothes were definitely an improvement, but it was still an uphill battle against the exhaustion waiting to claim her. "Officer?" She laid her hand against his cheek and his good eye slowly opened. In the light of the lamp she could see now that his eyes were a bright sky blue. "How're you doing?"

He managed to barely nod his head again.

With the door shut, the fire had heated the room to a cozy temperature. "You ought to be warm in no time. You've got a cut over your eye I need to clean. Okay?''

He nodded again, and she gathered the things she needed from Jared's bathroom. He flinched as she dabbed at the dried blood caked over his bruised eye, and she jumped back. ''I'm sorry, I didn't mean to hurt you.''

''S'okay,'' he managed to whisper through his cracked lips.

She smiled at the effort he'd made and took a deep breath before resuming her task. The left side of his face was swollen and purple, and he had a cut on the corner of his bottom lip, as well as the one over his eye. Once she cleaned the blood away, he looked better. She applied an antiseptic ointment to his lip and his eye and pulled the cut over his eye closed with a butterfly bandage.

With gentle fingers she probed the back of his head to make sure he wasn't bleeding from the knock he'd taken from his own gun. She found a huge knot on the right side and gently explored it to make sure it wasn't bleeding. She sighed grate-fully when she realized it wasn't. His color was returning, and she sighed again when she realized that she could see no sign of any dangerous white patches of frostbite on his face.

''What?'' he whispered as he searched her face with his good eye.

She forced herself to smile. ''You have a big

knot on your head, which means you probably have a concussion. Especially considering how long you were unconscious. The good news is you don't have frostbite on your face. I guess I'd better check your hands and feet.''

She eased the covers back along his side and pulled out his left hand. The skin was red and chapped-looking, but had no sign of white any- where. His knuckles were raw, and it took her a moment to realize that it was from fighting rather than the cold. She smoothed some antiseptic on both his hands and put a pair of Jared's wool socks on his feet after she determined that they were fine as well. Her fingers brushed against his boxer shorts, and now that life was returning to her own hands, she realized that his shorts were wet as well.

''Oh man,'' she whispered under her breath as a high color swept up her face. She looked up to find the officer staring at her with a hard look in his eye. It came to her then that he still didn't trust her. After all she'd done for him, he was still ex- pecting the worst. She jumped up and cleared her throat. ''Your boxer shorts are wet too. My hands were so cold, I didn't realize it before.''

The glare in his good eye died to be replaced with what looked like relief, but she couldn't be sure. The blankets shifted as he moved, and she turned away to stoke the fire. All she could think was *thank goodness he's removing them him-*

self. She could have pretended for a lifetime and never come up with a situation this tense and awkward. She was probably lucky he didn't have his gun. He might have shot her before she could have explained anything.

The one good thing was now she had a viable excuse to tell Jared. Her eldest brother wasn't much for mulling over how fate worked, but saving someone's life was surely worth being stupid enough to get caught in a storm. At least it sounded good at the moment. Her decision to keep Blaze even had some reinforcement now. Although he'd be sure to point out that she wouldn't have been out there if weren't for the thrill of riding such a well-trained horse. She sighed as she wiggled her toes against the warmth of the fire; winning an argument with Jared had never happened in her lifetime, and she really didn't expect to anytime soon.

The tingle in her hands and feet began to fade, and her eyes were drooping while she swayed on her feet beside the fire. She shook her head to clear it as she tried to remember what she had to do now. The officer's underwear was lying beside the bed while the man himself was lying quietly with both eyes closed. At least his shivering had stopped.

Her heart stopped for a moment and then began beating furiously. What if he was lying too quietly? Her steps were jerky as she crossed the room and reached out to find his pulse. His skin was warm under her fingertips, and she knew he was still alive even before she found his steady pulse. Her fingers were shaking, and she twisted them together as she bit her lip.

The guy deserved better than this. He rated several doctors and a nice hospital bed at the very least after what he'd been through. Geez, how stupid could she be? They'd been in the house for at least an hour and she hadn't even thought to call for help. There was a phone on the nightstand beside Jared's bed, and she grabbed for it.

Total silence. She popped the button several times, but there wasn't any hope of getting a dial tone. Her spirits sank as she replaced the receiver. She glanced over at her patient and drew back sharply when she found his gaze on her.

"Um . . . I'm sorry. The phone's out too. I should have thought to check it first thing, but I didn't think of it." The lamp cast a soft light that warmed his complexion to a pale beige. She was glad to see him looking better, but the look in his eye unnerved her. Her imagination worked overtime as she pictured what he was thinking. More than likely he thought she had cut the phone line and checked the phone only for his benefit.

"Doesn't sound like they could get here anyway," he answered in a soft whisper. He winced as he moved his jaw and slowly pulled his hand out to run it over the bruises on the side of his face.

"Um . . . no, I guess not." Having him be so calm after she'd expected him to accuse her of kidnapping him left her feeling out of her depth. They hadn't given classes in high school on how to handle an injured policeman. If they had, she probably wouldn't have remembered the instructions anyway. School was seven years in her past and most of what she'd learned then was a hazy fog now.

Her parents had retired from ranching the year she had graduated, and her brothers Jared and Paul had taken over the whole operation. They had five hundred acres to manage, plus they leased government land for grazing their cattle. It had been an easy transition for her brothers. Jared had been twenty-five at the time and Paul had been twenty-two. They both had college educations in agriculture and were more than ready to take over the reins. Her parents had moved to Sun City in Arizona, and it was only Sydney who had been at loose ends.

She was four years younger than Paul and had still been considered a baby even though she had just graduated from high school. Her family had expected her to go to college as well, but she'd had different ideas. She'd been riding horses since she was old enough to walk. When other kids her age were just getting involved in sports, she already had several years of competing under her belt. She started out barrel racing and pole bending, speed events on horseback that were judged solely on time. From there she had moved on to roping, and she still competed in jackpot team roping whenever she got a chance.

Once she got out of school her plan was to train horses. No one could deny that she had an uncanny ability with animals, and it was just a natural progression in her life to make a living at training. It had required money to get started, but eventually she had talked Jared into letting her use one pasture and the barn until she'd built up the business she had today. She had a reputation in the area now and always had a barn full of horses to work with. She concentrated on roping, cutting, and reining and turned out some of the best trained horses in the state.

Calf roping was a rodeo event that required a well-trained animal to anticipate every move of the calf and then keep the rope taut once the calf had been snared. One of her horses had been used by the champion in the Pro Rodeo Cowboys' Association finals in Las Vegas, and that feat had cemented her reputation. She had yet to train a champion in barrel racing, but she hoped she would someday.

Jared had never had cause to regret his decision to back her when she'd first started, and except for his being angry about Blaze, the two of them got along great. Which was just as well since they lived together in the large two-story ranch house that they'd grown up in. Paul had married just after Sydney had graduated from high school, and he and his wife lived a mile away in a small house they had built not far from the creek. He and Shannon had a two-year-old boy named Kolt, and thankfully they'd lifted the pressure about grandchildren from Jared and Sydney. Which was just as well since Jared and Sydney were so caught up in their work that they never took the time to date. They kept each other company, and what they had was enough. Anyway, it had been for the last seven years.

The only time Sydney socialized with other people was when she was selling a horse or agreeing to train one. She traveled to several rodeos a year to meet people and keep her name in the business, but other than that she spent all her time with her horses. Now having an officer in her brother's bed glaring at her was a little more than she knew what to do with.

"Um . . . how do you feel? I mean, can I get you anything?"

"You mean other than feeling like I've been run over by a Mack truck?"

The distrust seemed to be gone, but maybe he was just playing along with her and hoping to survive until the weather improved. She smiled faintly at his attempt at humor. "Yeah, other than that."

"I think I'll be okay. It's a lot better being warm. Thank you."

The look in his good eye was soft now, and she stepped back in confusion. Even with swelling on one side of his face, he was way too handsome. His dark hair was curling in a sexy, disorganized kind of way, and the vulnerability of his situation pulled at her. Feeling sorry for him wasn't going to do either one of them any good, and she refused to be attracted to him. He probably had a wife and a couple of kids anyway.

That thought bolstered her confidence and her face brightened. "You're welcome, officer."

"Mark."

Sydney lifted her eyebrows in confusion. "I'm sorry?"

"My name is Mark. Mark Adams."

"Oh. Well. Um . . . I guess that's a good sign. I mean, that you remember your name. Maybe your concussion isn't that bad. Do you feel dizzy or nauseated or anything?"

Definitely, to both questions, but he wasn't going to admit it to this angel standing in front of him. He didn't know if angels had human-looking brown hair with streaks of gold in it or not, but he was sure she was an angel. Even though her hair was frizzing around her head in disarray and most of the time her green eyes looked uncertain, he knew. No woman of her size was strong enough to throw him over a horse, and he did remember being on a horse. The image had faded in and out, and it had taken him a long time to recognize that rocking motion, but it had definitely been a horse. And since no one else seemed to be around, she had to be the one who had gotten him up on its back. In other words, she had to be an angel. Sent specifically to save his life.

He'd been afraid of her at first. He'd never seen an otherworldly being before. The fright in her own eyes had calmed him until the lights had gone out. The sudden darkness had startled him into believing he'd gone blind, until she'd shined the flashlight at him. Once she'd turned that halo of light on herself, he'd been sure about her. He didn't know why he rated such good treatment, but he wasn't about to argue with it.

The timeline of events was just a little fuzzy in his mind, but he did remember being confused by how human she looked. She didn't have wings or a halo, but maybe angels were supposed to be disguised as humans. Made them more approachable—easier to accept. Even though her hair was a mess and her figure was distorted by the baggy sweats she wore, he thought she was the most beautiful angel-woman he'd ever seen. Her voice was soft and husky, and it dripped down his nerve endings like warm honey. His thoughts began to fade and he forgot to answer her question as his eyes gradually closed.

Chapter Three

Sydney gazed down at him as she watched his face glide into relaxation. He almost had a trusting look about him, but that couldn't be right. The concussion he had was probably just sucking the energy right out of him. Once he felt better, he'd be accusing her of who-knew-what. He'd probably even arrest her or something. Conspiracy to help an attempted murder or whatever the legal jargon was.

Of course it was possible that he just wasn't that lucid, which made his distrust perfectly natural. Maybe he'd get over it by morning. Actually maybe he'd already gotten over it. He had thanked her after all. Well, only time would tell.

A log in the fire crumbled and fell to the side,

and she shook her head as reality returned. There were still plenty of things to do before she could rest and standing around pondering the mysteries of her patient wasn't getting her anywhere. There was no telling how long the storm would last, which meant she'd have to conserve all the firewood in the house. Because there would be only one fire, she was going to have to sleep in this room as well.

The beam of the flashlight illuminated a small path in front of her as she opened the door and headed out into the cold hallway. The frigid temperature jump-started her brain into action and her sluggish steps picked up as she headed down to the basement again. No one in her family had gone camping since her parents had moved away, but all their gear was still organized neatly on the wooden shelves lining the far wall at the bottom of the staircase. A two-inch foam pad rested upright against one unfinished cement wall, and a dark brown, down-filled sleeping bag was in easy reach on the top shelf. She stuffed the bag under her arm while she held the flashlight in her hand. The pad in her other hand trailed along behind her as she trekked back to Jared's room.

The heat in the room blasted her in the face when she opened the door, and she shivered against the luxurious feel of it on her skin. The officer was still lying with his eyes closed, and she decided to let him rest while she spread out her own bed in front of the fireplace. There was plenty of wood stacked by the wall, and after placing another log on the fire she lay down. The warmth of the room was too tempting to resist, and even though there were still plenty of things to do, she closed her eyes.

Awakening slowly, she gazed up at the ceiling and tried to remember where she was. The air was cool, and as she reached out to pull the covers over her, she realized she wasn't in her own bed. Then it hit her. With a quick glance she checked the policeman who was still lying on his back covered knee-deep in comforters. The lantern beside the bed provided enough light that he was easy to see. She could tell by the color of his skin that he was still alive and breathing.

The fire had died down while she was asleep. While moving to get another log she brought her watch up to her face. It was only midnight, but she felt as refreshed as if she'd been sleeping all night. Her stomach rumbled with an ominous growl as she stoked the flames to a higher heat. Her last meal had been at least twelve hours ago, and after the strenuous afternoon she'd had it was no wonder she was starving.

Before she could do anything about a meal, she had to check on the officer. She didn't remember any specifics from her first aid class in high school, but she had watched rescue shows on TV, and she vaguely recalled something about waking a person with a concussion every two hours. It didn't sound like anything that would hurt in any case.

Lightly touching her fingers to his throat assured her that his pulse was still strong and steady. She shook his shoulder gently, and his eyelids fluttered and opened with a snap. She knew she should check his pupils but didn't recall what she was supposed to look for. "How're you doing, officer?" she whispered instead.

He frowned as he tried to think. He'd seen this woman before . . . and then he remembered. "Hi, angel."

His voice wasn't much more than a croak, and Sydney's heart started knocking against her breastbone. He was delirious. Oh no. Did that mean his brain was swelling? Oh man, what was she supposed to do?

The terror in her eyes woke him like nothing else could, and the rest of his memory came tumbling back. However, why she was so afraid eluded him. "What's the matter?"

"Um . . ." Sydney tried to organize her thoughts as she frantically twisted her fingers together. "Um . . . you tell me. Do you feel sick?"

A carpenter had set up shop in the back of his head and was busily hammering away, but other than that he didn't feel that bad. The nausea had passed, for which he was thankful. ''I've got a few aches and pains, I guess.''

Sydney was surprised at his calm demeanor. ''What's your name?''

He remembered telling her that once, but obediently he answered, ''Mark Adams.''

She didn't really know if that was true or not, but at least it was consistent. ''What day is it?''

He frowned. ''The last I remember it was Wednesday.''

Her heart settled down and began beating more normally. ''What do you do for a living?''

''State trooper, but that's too easy of a question since you keep calling me officer.''

She smiled and weakly sank to the bed as her knees went limp. ''You're too smart for me.''

She was relaxed now, but he couldn't forget how afraid she'd been. ''Why did you look so scared?'' The wind was still howling against the windowpane, and it was too loud to tell if there was someone else moving around in the house. He pushed quickly to his elbows but immediately sank back against the pillows as a wave of dizziness washed over him.

His good color receded like a wave pulling away from the shore, and she spoke sharply in sudden concern. ''You shouldn't move, officer. You were hit over the head with the butt of a gun, you know.'' Warmth trickled back into his face as he rested back, and she lowered her voice. ''I was afraid you were having complications from being hit over the head, but you seem lucid enough. Or at least I thought so until you tried to sit up.''

''Sorry,'' Mark answered as he swallowed hard.

''Looks like you weren't quite ready for that move yet,'' she said more softly. ''Why don't you try to get some more sleep. It doesn't sound like we'll be able to get you out of here anytime soon anyway.''

''We?'' Mark asked as he carefully opened his eyes and looked around.

She knew it. He didn't trust her. He was just being friendly to find out more information. The first time she'd figured that out she'd been angry. After all she'd done to help him, it didn't seem fair that he thought she was a criminal. This time she wasn't angry—hurt was more like it. His sense of humor had gotten under her skin. She liked him enough already that his opinion bothered her. ''Yes, we,'' she answered. ''You and me. I got you here by myself, but getting you out would be much easier with your cooperation.''

''You're losing me.''

''We're four miles from the highway. This house is on a dirt lane that is covered with at least a foot of snow by now. The lane will have to be bladed before a vehicle can travel on it, which takes time. If you're capable of sitting up by the time the storm stops, I can get you to the highway on a snowmobile. My brother Paul has a cellular phone; we'll call when he comes and get you an ambulance or more police officers—whichever you prefer—to meet us out by the road.''

''How is Paul going to get here?''

''Snowmobile.'' She could see he was going to ask another question and answered before he could speak again. ''He only lives a mile away. He's even farther from the highway than we are, but he'll come up to check on me and get my help feeding the cattle.''

That made perfect sense and he relaxed against his pillows as he studied her face. He remembered thinking she was an angel the first time he'd seen her and then thinking she was an angel in disguise when he'd been able to focus better. His mind had cleared now, and he could see she was really human after all. She even had a brother who lived a mile away.

Her hair was tousled about her head every which way, but she was still the most beautiful woman he'd ever seen. He wanted to know everything about her, and he smiled as he realized that he had at least all night to get to know her better. The room he was in was decorated with dark oak furniture with a definite masculine touch, and he asked the most important question first. ''Whose room is this?''

She pushed to her feet sharply as she thought of answering: *attempted killer number one, two, or three—take your pick.* She swallowed that retort when she realized how easy it would be for him to arrest her. "My brother Jared uses this room. You're wearing his wool socks, as a matter of fact."

The honey had drained out of her voice to be replaced with a frosty tone, and he wondered what he'd said. He didn't wonder long before her answer registered. She had another brother. Nothing said about a husband yet. He smiled as wide as he could with a split in his lip. "I hope he won't mind."

Sydney's stomach rumbled again, and she stepped further back from the bed. "No, I'm sure he'll realize it was for a good cause."

"How come he's not here?"

"Because he's in Arizona visiting my parents. I only have two brothers. Jared and I live here alone. My brothers ranch. I train horses. My parents are retired. Anything else you want to know?"

She was angry, but all he could do was smile again. She wasn't married.

What he thought of as a smile looked more like a grimace to Sydney, and she wondered how much pain he was in. Even though he was giving her the third degree, she was still anxious about him. Aches and pains could be something more serious that he was just too stoic to talk about. "Are you sure you're okay? Not woozy or anything?"

Mark liked the way her brows drew together over her pale green eyes when she was concerned about him. If she didn't seem to be so afraid when she thought he was hurting, he'd be tempted to fake it a little bit. "I was only dizzy when I tried to sit up. My head hurts some and the side of my face, but I've had worse."

"You have?"

"I used to box in high school. Bruises on my face were a common sight then."

"Oh." For a minute she had expected him to say he'd been attacked many times while working as a cop. Boxing sounded much better. At least both people knew what they were doing and didn't intend to kill each other. Those kids out on the highway had been a different story all together.

Her stomach rumbled again. "I was going to put together some supper. Are you hungry?"

"No, not really."

"I suppose that's just as well. Eating probably isn't a good idea when you have a concussion." She stepped closer to the door. "Well, umm . . . why don't you try to sleep some more? I'll try not to disturb you while I'm cooking."

"Cooking? Without electricity?"

"Haven't you ever gone camping and cooked over an open fire?"

"No. . . . but I take it you have."

"Yes, I have. I'm just going to heat some soup, though."

"Over this fire?" All of a sudden it was important to him that he keep her in sight. He knew he'd worry about her if he couldn't see what she was doing.

"Yep. This blizzard could last for several days, and I think it's best if I conserve the firewood just in case." Oh man, what a stupid thing to say. Scaring the patient was the last thing you were supposed to do. And here she was talking as if they were about to run out of wood at any moment.

"Good idea."

The man was way too calm. No wonder he was a police officer. He obviously didn't rile easily. "Umm . . . Right. I'll be right back."

"Okay."

His voice sounded sleepy and unconcerned, and she turned her back as she closed the door behind her. One minute he was grilling her and the next he didn't seem to care. It must be the concussion. It was just making him sleepy. She, on the other hand, was wide awake. Her hands were trembling and she interlocked her fingers as she took a deep breath. He was going to be okay, and she didn't really think he'd arrest her. So no problem. She could handle this situation.

She didn't want to think about why her hands were still shaking as she moved off down the hall.

Away from the warm fire the blast of the storm was more noticeable. The windows were all frosted over, making it impossible to see out, but the wind was still shrieking at an intense level, and she knew the storm was far from over. The house was creaking and settling the way it did every day, but now that she was moving through it with just a flashlight for company, she was more than a little spooked.

The shadows at the edge of her little pool of light were wide and hulking, and they seemed to move in tandem with the creaking going on around her. She hated it when Jared went away overnight, but she'd die before she ever told him that. She always told herself there was nothing to be afraid of, but that never stopped her heart from palpitating at every little noise. She'd been in too much of a daze to notice it earlier, but now the creeps had moved in along her spine and were tapping out an eerie song on her nerve endings.

"This is ridiculous," she muttered as she jumped a mile when the top stair to the basement groaned as she put her weight on it. She needed an old pot to heat her soup in and she knew of a perfect one in their camping gear. It was blackened on the outside from sitting in many a fire and one more wouldn't hurt it any. Getting it was the only problem.

She'd feel better if Mark were walking along

with her, but at least he was here. Even if he didn't trust her and affected her in a way she didn't want to analyze, at least he was company. Being alone in this blizzard would be much worse. Her entire family was probably worried sick about her, but wouldn't they be surprised when they found out what she'd accomplished all by herself? Thinking about the praise she would receive made it easier to clink and clunk her way through the pots and pans in the basement and make it back to the kitchen to grab a can of soup. She raided the shelves for bread and cheese and a glass of milk before heading back to Jared's room.

Mark opened his good eye when he heard the door creak open. She tiptoed in without looking at him, and he smiled at her cat burglar imitation. It had been hard to stay awake while he waited for her to come back, but he'd wanted to make sure she was all right. "What are you making?"

Sydney jumped and her spoon dropped against the tray with a clatter. She'd dumped her soup in her pot and added water before leaving the kitchen. Everything else she'd carried on a tray.

"Sorry. Didn't mean to scare you."

Sydney turned toward him. "That's okay. I just thought you'd be asleep by now. Are you okay?"

"I've got a hard head. Stop worrying."

His voice was soft with concern and she wondered what he was up to. He shifted moods faster than the weather changed in Colorado. "It isn't every day that I drag a police officer back to my house in the middle of a huge snowstorm, you know. I've never been caught in one on horseback before, either."

The drowsiness Mark was feeling lifted with that statement. "You were caught in the storm?"

Sydney sighed as she set her heavy pot beside the fire to heat. She sat back on her sleeping bag and turned toward him. "Yes and no. I was out having a good time working with my favorite horse, and it started to snow before I realized the storm had come in. I was heading back and would have made it easily except I heard some gunshots." She shivered as she remembered the scene. "Anyway, I waited awhile for a passing motorist to help, but nobody drove by. I don't know if the storm stopped them or if it was just my bad luck that nobody was driving by at the time. The snow was falling thicker, and I couldn't wait any longer, so I threw you over my horse and pretty much gave Blaze his head. We wouldn't have made it without him. I had no clue what direction we were going."

Mark frowned. "Why not use my radio to call for help?"

"One of them drove off in your car."

Mark reached for his hip and then realized he wasn't wearing his uniform. "What about the one I was wearing?"

"There wasn't anything on your uniform." She could see he didn't believe her. Scrambling to her feet, she strode out into the hall and came back with his clothes. She held up his jacket and his shirt and pants. There was nothing there but the soft fabric.

"Are you sure it wasn't there? Wait, never mind," he said as he shook his head. "It works through the car radio. It's not any good without the car."

Sydney didn't answer as she thought back to everything she'd seen. The memory was still vivid in her mind. Just before the man with the gun had kicked the officer down the incline, he'd swung the gun belt over his head. "Was your radio on that gun belt thing you were wearing?"

Mark nodded. "Yes, but it doesn't matter. Even if I had it, it wouldn't work."

Wanting to set the record straight anyway, Sydney answered, "The guy that had your gun took it off you. He took it with him when he got in your car. It all happened so fast, I didn't know what to do. They didn't see me, and since I didn't have a gun, I didn't call attention to myself. It surprised me when he just kicked you down the slope and drove off. But when the snow got thicker, it was obvious they'd left you out there to freeze to death. No one driving by would have known you were there."

"And thanks to you, I'm as warm as a bear in hibernation."

Sydney draped his clothes over the small chair in the corner of the room by the fire. How could anybody be so blasé about such violence? It still made her sick when she thought about it, and she wasn't the one who'd been attacked. He must think she had something to do with it and was acting nonchalant to throw her off-guard or something. She swallowed hard against the rising in her stomach and affected a natural tone of voice. "Are you sure bears are warm when they're hibernating?"

He didn't have a clue, but he knew he didn't like the look of pain on her face when she'd remembered what she'd seen. When he'd first seen the expensive car going twenty miles an hour over the speed limit, he'd thought it was a rich kid out for a joyride. When the young driver had stepped out of the car before he'd even gotten out of his own vehicle, he'd been even more sure he'd assessed the situation correctly. The kid handed him his driver's license, and just when he'd barely glanced down at it the kid had sucker punched him.

If it had just been the one kid, he could have handled it easily, but the other two had jumped out and joined in. One of them had tried to take his gun, and while they were wrestling for possession of it, it had gone off and shot one of them in the leg. The rest of it wasn't clear. He'd radioed in where he'd stopped before he got out of the car, but from the sound of the storm no one would know what had happened to him. If it wasn't for this woman, he'd be dead, and he knew it.

He'd made a huge mistake in how he'd read the situation, and he could see the violence of the whole thing had shaken her badly. He was disgusted, sick, and scared about the whole thing, but he didn't have time to indulge himself in those emotions. Helping her to deal with it was more important. "Well, I've never actually seen a bear in hibernation before. Have you?"

"Can't say as I have. I think I'd take my chances with a bear over those three punks any day, though," she added as she bent to stir her soup. Her appetite had fled, but she didn't want him to know how upset his attitude was making her.

Mark didn't know what to say to ease her pain. Maybe there weren't words for situations like these. "Come to think of it, I might have been better off with the bear myself. I've never seen a bear try to drive before, though."

Sydney dropped the spoon in the pot and turned

to face him. "How can you make a joke out of something like that?"

The pain in her face squeezed the life right out of his heart, and his face paled. He closed his eye and turned away because he couldn't bear to see it. His mistake was the cause of her pain, and he would never forgive himself for that.

Sydney forgot about everything when she saw the color drain out of his cheeks. Oh man, not again. "Mark?" She reached his side in one large stride and felt for his pulse.

The soft contact of her fingers on his neck made him flinch. She slid her fingers lower and quickly found his pulse. "Mark? Mark, are you okay?"

"I'm fine," he mumbled without opening his eye. He kept his face averted as well. "I'm just tired, that's all. Just need to sleep."

"Are you sure that's all? Does your head hurt worse?"

"No. Just sleepy."

Sydney wasn't at all sure that he'd tell her if something was wrong. She'd never met a stronger, tougher man in her life. She'd thought her brothers were tough, but being attacked would definitely upset them. But that didn't seem to bother this man at all. Maybe cops were just a different breed altogether. "Please, Mark. I want you to tell me if you need anything."

He liked the sound of his name on her lips, but

he didn't deserve that kind of pleasure. "Just sleep," he mumbled again.

"Okay. All right. Get some rest. Maybe you'll feel better next time you wake up."

He didn't answer and she slowly backed away.

Chapter Four

After a while the color returned to his face, and she relaxed enough to eat a bowl of soup while she watched him sleep. His head was turned away from her, leaving the battered side of his face in clear view. The bumps and bruises were magnified in the soft lamplight, and she shuddered as she thought about what had been done to him. Now that she was rested and had eaten something, she realized how much danger she'd been in as well. If those men had seen her, they would have shot her. There was no doubt about that. They'd been erasing all traces of their presence by leaving Mark out there to freeze to death.

They'd never even glanced up the slight rise the lane took underneath the Carrigan sign. She'd been

so astonished, she hadn't thought to hide. It was
pure dumb luck that they hadn't seen her. Being
alone in a storm was not her idea of a good time,
but at least it would keep those punks from checking on their victim. The state patrol would have
closed the highway a long time ago due to the poor
conditions. There was no way those kids could get
out to her ranch.

That thought made it easier to sit and listen to
the groaning of the old house as it settled and
grumbled in the wind. Her father and brothers had
several rifles and shotguns in the house, but she'd
never even touched one. She shivered at the
thought. She could never kill an animal, and living
so far away from other people didn't give her any
opportunity to think about having a gun for protection. The storm was better security than a gun
in her hands would be any day, and she was glad
Mother Nature was on her side for once.

Her mind was racing with all kinds of thoughts,
making her way too wired to even think about
sleeping anymore. Every now and then she put another log on the fire and otherwise just sat mes-
merized by the dancing flames.

A soft rustling noise behind her made her turn.
"Are you okay, officer?" She asked as she saw
his eye was open and trained on her.

"Too hot," Mark mumbled through thick lips.
His tongue was sticking to the roof of his mouth
as if he'd just eaten a spoonful of peanut butter.

Sydney hurried over and peeled three of the comforters back to the foot of the bed. There was a glass in the bathroom, and she filled it with cool water and brought it back to him. She sat next to him and slid her hand under his shoulders to prop him up before raising the glass to his lips.

While he was taking small sips, her brain was registering the feel of his smooth skin against her forearm and the heavy weight of his head against her shoulder. Her heartbeat instantly accelerated, but she did her best to hide it from him.

"Okay," he said when he'd drunk about half the glass.

She eased him back down and slid off the bed to get away from him. She cleared her throat before turning back toward him.

"Is that better?"

"Yeah. Thanks," he added almost as an afterthought.

"Do you still know who you are or should I go through the question thing again?"

He hesitated as he wiped his forehead with one hand. "I'm okay. What time is it?"

Sydney glanced at her watch. "It's almost three o'clock."

"In the morning?"

"I guess you can call it that. Seems more like the middle of the night to me."

"Is it still snowing?"

"I don't know for sure. I can't see out any of the windows. It's still blowing hard, though. Even if it's not snowing, it's gotta be a white-out out there."

Mark nodded as the smell of chicken soup wafted across the room. "Did you eat your dinner?"

"Um . . . yeah. Why, do you want some?"

His tongue was moving more freely in his mouth now, but the thought of food didn't sound too good. "No, thanks."

"Do you want something else to drink? Juice maybe?"

"No, not right now." He glanced up at her worried face. "I'm going to be fine, you know. You can stop worrying so much."

Sydney twisted her fingers together as she took a step back and shrugged her shoulders. "Sorry, I can't help it."

Mark made an effort to wave his hand at her. "It's all right. I just don't like to see you looking so concerned, that's all. Makes me feel guilty."

"Guilty?"

"Yeah," he answered as he rubbed his good eye. "It's my fault you're dealing with all this. I'm sorry."

Sydney's mouth dropped open as she scrambled to think of something to say. He was sorry? That didn't make sense. Didn't he think she was in on the plot to kidnap him? What did he mean he was sorry?

"I don't blame you for being angry. I would be too if I were you," he added.

"Um . . . I'm not angry. I'm . . . well, really, it's not your fault. You don't have anything to be sorry for."

"Pretty rookie mistake taking my eyes off that kid. Somebody like you shouldn't have to witness stuff like that."

"I, uh, didn't see the whole thing. I'd say from what I saw that they'd already planned to jump you whenever they could. Three against one is hardly fair."

"Are you defending me?"

"Well, yes. You seem to need it, since you're so busy blaming yourself. And what do you mean, somebody like me shouldn't see stuff like that?"

For a moment Mark couldn't think of anything to say. "I just meant that a young woman like you shouldn't be exposed to violence like that."

"Oh. Well, I got us both back here, so I must be tougher than you're giving me credit for."

"I don't know any women strong enough to throw me over a horse. Believe me, I'm not questioning how tough you are."

"Oh," she answered again. There were plenty of women police officers who witnessed violence every day, which made his statement all the more confusing. Why was she any different in his mind? "Are you against women as police officers then?"

Mark's brows drew together. "No, not specifically. Why?"

Sydney planted her hands on her hips and shifted her weight to one foot. "I'm sure there are young policewomen on the force. Are they exempt from witnessing violence just because they're women?"

Mark chuckled until the motion awakened some stiff muscles in his side, making him stop. "You think I'm being sexist, don't you?" He didn't wait for her to answer. "I didn't mean it that way. Cops are trained for that kind of thing, you know. I get the impression you haven't seen that much violence in your life, and I just meant to say I'm sorry for being the cause of it this time."

"Oh." Now she'd put her foot in it and there wasn't a graceful way to retrieve it. She scrubbed at her face with her hands as she sighed. "I'm sorry. I guess I don't understand someone like you at all." This situation was too awkward for words, and for the first time she started hoping the storm would end soon.

"Someone like me?" Mark asked with a small smile.

Sydney dropped her hands. Nothing she said came out right. And then she saw the smile on his face. "Uh-uh. We're not going there."

"Why not? I want to hear what you think of someone like me."

"Right. You know, you're as hard to win a conversation with as Jared is."

"That's an interesting outlook. Do you always try to win conversations? And how do you go about doing that anyway?"

Sydney couldn't help it as she broke out laughing. "Now you're making fun of me, aren't you?"

Her laughter washed over him like a soft shower, and he had to suppress a shiver of pleasure. "No, I'd never do that."

The warm look in his eye was infectious, and she smiled wider. "Yeah, right. How did we get onto this subject anyway?"

Mark shrugged in answer. "I'll let it drop for now, if you tell me why you never win a conversation with Jared."

Sydney retreated to her makeshift bed on the floor and sat down. "Because he never lets me, I guess."

"Nope, not good enough."

With a hearty sigh, she pretended to protest against his slave driver attitude. "You'd have to meet him to understand. He's smart for one thing and too stubborn for his own good for another. I've been right lots of times; he just won't admit it."

"He sounds like an arrogant brute."

Sydney laughed again. "Doesn't he, though."

Laughing some more, she added. "He's not—a brute, I mean, or arrogant—either one. He's really quite wonderful, if you want to know the truth. Mostly he pretends to be a bully, but he's a real softie underneath. I hope he's not driving Mom and Dad crazy, worrying about this storm. He's supposed to fly home tomorrow, but it doesn't look like he's going to make it now."

The love in her eyes as she thought about her brother made Mark's heart squeeze. There was no one in his life who looked like that when thinking about him, and all of a sudden he realized what he'd been missing. "If you never win, how do you know he's a softie?" he asked to get her talking again. The soft look about her had him captivated, and he didn't want her to lose it yet.

"Well, I never win the argument, but that doesn't mean I don't win the war. I'm not a complete pushover, you know."

"Hmmm. Prove it."

She narrowed her eyes as she focused on him. His doubts about her weren't very flattering, but he looked like he was just teasing. At this point she'd give him the benefit of the doubt. "The horse I was riding today is a perfect example. Blaze is the best horse in the world. I got him when he was only a year old. The man who owned him couldn't do a thing with him, mostly because the guy was an idiot."

Mark smiled at the disgust in her voice. "Blaze is the smartest horse I've ever worked with. It was love at first sight, and even though I've had several offers for him, I've never been able to sell him. Jared was livid when he found out about the first offer. He thought I'd never make it in the horse training business if I couldn't sell any of my horses. I use Blaze in lots of ways to help me train my other horses, and I told Jared, Blaze is the only one I'm hanging onto. Jared tried to threaten me, but we both knew he didn't really mean it. I've sold several horses I've started since then, plus who knows how many that I've taken for my regular clients. I think I've made my point; and after Blaze saved your life today, I don't think Jared will say anything more about it."

To Mark it sounded as if he were going to have a huge fight on his hands whenever Jared did come home. Keeping his beloved sister out in a blizzard wasn't going to earn Mark any brownie points with him.

"What about you?" Sydney asked as she saw the thoughtful expression on his face. "Do you have family around here?"

"Just my father. He lives in Boulder."

"You don't have brothers or sisters?"

"Nope. I'm an only child. My mother lives in California."

Sydney raised her eyebrows, but she hated to ask the most obvious question.

Mark sighed. "My parents divorced a long time ago. She's remarried now, but my Dad isn't."

"I'm sorry."

This concern she kept showing him was getting addictive. "Like I said, it was a long time ago. I was in high school then."

"How old are you now?"

"Twenty-seven." He smiled. "Am I allowed to ask the same question?"

Seeing him smile made her feel better, and she smiled back. "Well, you're positively ancient compared to me."

"Am I old enough to be your father?"

Laughter cascaded out of her as she rocked back on her bed. "Not quite."

"Hmmm, let's see. You've got your own business, so how about twenty-two?"

"You're definitely warmer."

"Do I get a prize if I get it right?"

"A swift kick in the butt, maybe," Sydney said with a mock sneer. "Oh, all right. I'm twenty-five."

"Twenty-five?" Mark could pretend horror as well as the next person. "You're definitely over the hill. It's a slow slide down the back side from here, that's for sure."

Sydney laughed again and wondered where the awkwardness had gone. "Well, you oughtta know. Old man," she muttered under her breath.

Mark tried not to laugh. "I'm not going to win this conversation, am I?"

Sydney fought to control her expression. "Giving up already?"

"I'm no Jared, I guess."

"Good thing. One of him's enough." That sobered her. "I bet they're all pacing the floor right now. Paul will have told them how bad the storm is, and they'll all be worried sick that I'm here all alone."

"Except you're not alone."

An unexpected smile lit her face. "No, I guess not. You know, I hate being here by myself. I couldn't get away right now, or I would have gone with Jared to Arizona. I never sleep that well when I'm the only one in the house."

"How come?" Mark asked as he rolled onto his side, propping his head on his arm.

Sydney shrugged. "I know it's dumb, but I can't help it. All the noises suddenly become more sinister when I'm here alone."

"And who says there's never a police officer around when you need one?"

The laughter came from deep inside her. First her stomach began to jiggle, then her shoulders wiggled until the merriest sound he'd ever heard tumbled from her lips. He had to laugh too, and he didn't even notice the discomfort in his side or the split in his lip.

When she could talk again she answered with a little more seriousness. "I'm glad you're doing better. You had me worried there for a while."

There were several things Mark wanted to say to that, but he hesitated. Effusive praise would make things awkward between them again, and more than anything he didn't want that to happen. For now he'd go for halfway in-between. "You handle yourself well in a crisis. Are you sure you're not a nurse in disguise?"

"Nope. No Florence Nightingales around here. Common sense is the best you get."

"Too bad they can't bottle common sense. It'd sell like a house on fire, and a lot of people need to buy it."

Sydney studied his face for a moment. "You see people at their worst in your job, don't you?"

"A lot of the time, yes." He knew it wasn't what she wanted to hear, but he couldn't lie to her.

"Why do you do it?"

Mark took a deep breath before answering. "I'm not sure there's an easy answer to that, except maybe—somebody has to do it."

She hadn't meant to pry, but she could see the question had been too personal. A tactful retreat was necessary. "I've always admired police officers. More because I know I could never do that job, and it so impresses me that people like you can. Your profession takes such a bad rap nowadays, and I can't help thinking what a weak excuse that is. No one wants to take responsibility for their own actions anymore. It's always someone else's fault. I think it's sick.''

Mark blinked in surprise. That was the last thing he had expected her to say. ''I don't hear too many people outside my profession talk like that anymore, but it's nice to hear. Thanks.''

Sydney shrugged and then lit up with a smile. ''How many people do you associate with outside your profession?''

That stopped him and he had to think before he could answer. ''Not very many, I guess.''

''Your family?''

''Just my mother, but I really don't see her that often anymore. My dad works for the Boulder County Sheriff's Department.''

She'd been fishing to see if he really did have a wife and kids, but he hadn't taken the bait. ''Don't you have other family? Cousins, uncles, a wife?''

''Yes, yes, and no, but I only see them at Christmas and usually that's not every year.''

She raised her eyebrows. ''Christmas isn't every year?''

He had to smile. ''I don't see them every year at Christmas.''

''Oh.'' She drew the word out as she made her mouth big and round, still pretending that she hadn't understood him the first time. "That's too bad. How come you don't?"

She went through expressions faster than a woman going through her closet as she tried to decide what to wear, and he loved it. Her eyes had an emerald sparkle and a healthy pink glow splashed across her cheekbones, making an overall picture of such vitality that he couldn't remember the last time he'd seen such a pretty face. He knew he could watch her forever and never get tired of the view. "They don't all live around here and they have families of their own now. I have to work sometimes. I don't know—we get together when we can."

She nodded at that reasoning as she tried to come up with a tactful way to ask why he wasn't married.

He interrupted her thoughts. "So, what about you? You've talked about your immediate family, but do you have cousins, uncles, a husband?"

"No, no, and no. Both of my parents were only children, which is why they had three of us. They didn't want us to grow up alone."

"And why isn't a beautiful lady like you married with kids of her own?"

No one had ever described her as being beautiful, and she knew she looked a mess after the day she'd had. "I think there's something wrong with your vision. Do you normally wear glasses? Or maybe it's just that you only have one eye at the moment.''

He shook his head. ''I can see just fine.''

Sydney smiled. He was teasing her again. ''I guess I've been too busy with my own life to share it with anybody.''

''I know what you mean,'' Mark admitted.

''You've never been married?''

''No.'' He'd seen what the job could do to a marriage. He'd witnessed it in his mother all his life. Putting a woman through that was the last thing he wanted to do.

His face closed down, and she wondered what kind of woman could hurt him like that. She'd had a few casual dates in high school, but she'd never met anyone worth more of an effort, and after looking at his face she was glad. It looked like it hurt too much.

''I'm probably keeping you up too long,'' she said to break the sudden silence. ''I'm sure your body needs a lot of rest at this point. Maybe the wind will have let up by the next time you wake up.''

He came out of his memories to focus on her again. ''Aren't you going to get any sleep tonight?''

''Oh,'' she said as she smoothed her hands over her sleeping bag. ''I slept for a while earlier. I'm not that sleepy now.''

"You don't have to stay awake to watch me. I'm fine now. Really."

"Yes, you sure seem to be, but that's not why I'm awake."

"Is it the storm?"

How did he know that? She shrugged in response. "I've got most of my horses out in the pasture. I didn't have time to bring them in, and there're my brothers' cattle too. I can't help worrying about them, but if I get sleepy I'll lay down."

"This isn't the easiest life either, is it?"

"It's hard work, if that's what you mean. And battling nature in one way or another is stressful, but working for yourself and setting your own hours is such a free lifestyle. I could never live in town and go to a nine-to-five job every day."

"Staying up all night worrying doesn't help anything, though."

She sighed. "Will you try to sleep, if I try to sleep?"

"I'll close my eyes if you do."

She smiled at how silly they sounded as she slid under her sleeping bag and lay on her back. "Happy now?"

"No, your eyes are still open."

She scrunched her eyelashes together and tried not to laugh. "Is this better?"

"You look like you're in pain."

Sydney's eyes flashed open in outrage as she laughed in spite of herself. She looked around for something to throw and delighted in the deep chuckle coming from him. She couldn't find anything soft enough, and finally in frustration she pulled off her slipper and threw it instead.

Mark closed his eye and ducked as the slipper flew over his head, smacking into the wall behind him. ''You need to work on your aim.''

She pulled off her other slipper and let it fly with more precision. It hit him in the shoulder and slid down his side. ''Ouch,'' he complained as he rubbed his arm underneath the covers.

''You deserved it,'' she answered as she lay back down.

''It was worth it.''

His voice was soft and held a note she didn't recognize. ''You like having things thrown at you, you mean?''

He smiled. ''I meant it was worth it to hear you laugh.''

That got her attention and she studied him more closely.

It was getting harder to believe he was just teasing when he had such a caring look about him. ''Good night, officer.'' She rolled onto her side away from him and stared unseeingly at the fire.

''Good night, Angel.''

She rolled back to face him. "My name is Sydney."

He didn't answer as a small smile lifted the corners of his mouth. Slowly he closed his eye and relaxed.

Chapter Five

A strong gust of wind rattled the windowpane, and Sydney's eyes snapped open as her heart began to pound. The window shook again, and she breathed a sigh of relief as she recognized the familiar sound. There was more light in the room now, and she sat up to look at her watch. She hadn't expected to fall asleep at all, making it all the more surprising that it was eight o'clock in the morning.

The fire had burned down to hot embers, and the temperature in the room had cooled off considerably. As quietly as she could, she stoked it back up and added two more logs until the fire began to burn brightly again. Her stomach rumbled with a loud insistence that reminded her she hadn't eaten enough in the last twenty-four hours.

Both of her slippers were still on the bed, and she gently plucked them up without disturbing Mark. He was breathing deeply and regularly, which reassured her quite a bit. She still found herself half-expecting him to have a relapse.

The floorboards creaked as she moved to the door, but Mark didn't stir, and she opened the door and went out into the cold hallway. Hot oatmeal and toast sounded heavenly, and she hurried to gather everything she needed from the kitchen. She got an extra bowl, just in case Mark decided he was hungry, before heading back to the warmth of Jared's room.

The wind was still whistling and howling, and she didn't bother to look outside. A ground blizzard was just as bad as falling snow, and either way she and the officer were stuck inside until it stopped.

The warmth in the room made her shiver, and she hurried over next to the fireplace. The utensils clattered as she set the tray on the floor, and she winced. Glancing over her shoulder, she saw Mark rubbing his eye. "I'm sorry, did I wake you?"

He groaned as he rolled onto his back. "What time is it?"

"It's early. You can sleep some more if you want."

His bruised eye opened a tiny crack when he looked over at her. "Are you cooking again?"

"Yes, I'm quite the gourmet chef. My specialty this morning is oatmeal and toast. Want some?"

"That orange juice looks good."

"Really?" She stopped what she was doing and carried the glass to him. The thought of touching him again made her hand tremble, and it took a sheer force of will to steady it and pretend propping him up was no big deal. She stuffed a couple of extra pillows under his shoulders and then used both hands to help him drink.

He was taking it slowly to test his stomach, and after a few sips she put the glass on the nightstand. "Want to try a piece of toast?"

His bruised eye opened a little more as he arched his eyebrows. "Toast?"

"You're such a skeptic. I'll do my best not to burn it, but it might not get all that toasted either. Now hot water for oatmeal, I can do."

"If you say so."

She ignored him as she went back to preparing breakfast. She had a small bread-cooling rack that she intended to put close enough to the fire to make toast, and she already had a teakettle full of water sitting as close as she dared. She poured a generous heaping of oatmeal in her bowl and just a little bit in his before putting two pieces of bread on her rack and watching it like a hawk.

The bread ended up with charcoal stripes from the rack that made it look like a referee's uniform. The white strips in between weren't toasted, but it was the best she could do. She held up one piece. "Want to try?"

"Will you be mortally offended if I don't?"

She laughed softly. "No, that just leaves more for me."

"I think you need it more than I do."

"Hmmph." She wasn't going to answer that, and she buttered her toast while she waited for the water to heat. She was so hungry it tasted quite good, and she put two more slices on her rack.

"How is it?" Mark asked.

Sydney swallowed what she was chewing. "Are you changing your mind?"

"No, I don't think so."

Sydney rolled her eyes. "It's just bread, for heaven's sake." The teakettle began to whistle, and she pulled it away from the fire with a hot pad. Steam rose up and hit her in the face as she poured it over her oatmeal, and the aroma made her mouth water. She made sure his oatmeal was thin enough that he could digest it easily before taking it over to him.

The covers had slipped down, baring the top half of his chest. Both of his hands were lying on top of the comforter, and she noticed he'd drunk the rest of his juice while she'd been busy. The sight of the smooth muscles in his upper body made her swallow hard as she forced herself to look up and keep her gaze on his face.

She handed him the bowl, and he held on to it with one hand while he manipulated the spoon with the other. His coordination was good, and she breathed another sigh of relief. ''You look a lot better this morning,'' she said as she watched him take a tiny bite. The taste seemed to agree with him and a smile of pleasure lit his face as he swallowed.

''Mmm. That's good.''

He seemed to be all right on his own, and she retreated once again to her own bed. One bowl didn't even put a dent in her hunger, and she poured another one. After four pieces of toast and two bowls, she was finally satisfied.

Sydney looked up to find him watching her. ''Do you always eat such a big breakfast?'' he asked.

She looked down and brushed the crumbs off her sleeping bag. ''No, but I usually eat a decent dinner the night before. A bowl of soup isn't a decent dinner for me. Did you get enough?''

The empty juice glass and the remains of his oatmeal were sitting on the nightstand beside the bed. ''Yes, thanks. It was good; I just couldn't eat any more.''

''Well, let me know when you get hungry again.''

He nodded. "You know, I thought women only picked at their food. How come you can get away with eating like that?"

She knew he was teasing her again. "I work hard. Riding horses is good exercise, didn't you know?"

"If you're anything to go by, I can see."

She flushed and looked away. Trying to get on an even keel, she said, "I thought police officers ate doughnuts and were fat. How come you're not?"

"Touché," he said with a laugh.

"You must work out, huh?"

"Yeah, I go to a gym to lift. It gives me a chance to associate with people who aren't cops."

She smiled as she remembered asking him how many non-police officers he knew. "Where do you live?"

"In Fort Collins." He paused for a moment to study her. "Are we playing twenty questions again?"

Color rose in her face, even though he'd said it softly. "I'm sorry. I guess it isn't any of my business."

"Don't be sorry. I was kind of hoping we were because then I could ask you some more things."

"Oh? Like what?"

"Maybe it would be easier if you just told me about yourself."

Sydney shrugged. "I've told you just about everything already. I train horses for a living and this is where I live." She spread her hands out to encompass the entire room.

Mark shook his head. "There's got to be more than that. How come you and your brothers live here and your parents live in Arizona?"

Looking down to pluck at her sleeping bag, she sighed. "My Dad developed arthritis. He fought through it for years, but Mom got him to go with her to visit some friends of theirs who had retired to Arizona, and I guess the climate really agreed with him. The cold, biting wind around here never helped him any in the winter, and they finally made the decision to retire. He's taken up woodworking for something to do, and you wouldn't believe how good he is at it. He takes his time since his hands still bother him some, but he's made some really beautiful pieces. None of us were sure that he'd be happy away from his ranch, but he's surprised us all. I guess he was in more pain than he admitted."

Mark could tell that she really missed her parents, and her father especially. "So you and your brothers took over?"

"My brothers took over," she answered as she looked up. "My horses are separate, and I pay Jared and Paul for the use of the barn and one pasture."

"Hmmm."

She could tell what he was thinking from the look on his face. "I don't pay them in money, though. I just help them when they need it. Like when the storm ends, Paul and I will be out taking hay to all the cattle and blading the road and stuff. I'll have to take hay to my horses too. They're all out in the pasture right now. I hope they're okay."

Mark raised his eyebrows. "Why wouldn't they be?"

"Well, there's an open barn out there for them to get a break from the wind, but they won't have anything to eat. They won't go out of the barn to forage for grass in this kind of storm. They've got to be hungry." She sighed and dropped her hands in her lap. "I hate that."

"Surely they can go a couple days without food?"

"Yeah, I just don't want them to. Don't you have any animals you worry about? A dog or a cat?"

Mark shook his head. "I'm not home that much. It'd be cruel to expect an animal to hang out alone most of the time, so I've never gotten one. I would like to have a dog though."

Sydney's eyes lit with an inner glow as their conversation shifted to her favorite subject. "Paul has three dogs. They're all purebred German shepherds. He's also got a whole batch of puppies. Maybe you'd like to pick one out for yourself?"

Mark smiled at her enthusiasm. "Sounds nice, but I really don't have time for a puppy. It needs so much attention to turn into a good dog."

"That's true," Sydney admitted as her shoulders slumped. Then an idea hit her. "I've heard of cops that have dogs on the job. Why can't you be one of those?"

"There's only so many of those dogs to go around, and it takes special training, you know. I guess I've never seriously thought about it."

Sydney didn't know anything about training a dog for police work, but she could handle training one for gentleness and obedience. She'd helped Paul train several of his over the years before he sold them for good prices. Maybe she could train one for Mark. She could do the groundwork, and then Mark could take the dog to a specialist and have it trained for police work. Then the dog could go with him night and day.

Her animals had enriched her life so much, she couldn't imagine what it would be like not to have a pet. She'd feel a lot better if Mark had one, and the thought of giving him a dog fired her with excitement. Of course, she might never see Mark again after the storm was over. There wouldn't be any reason for them to keep in touch. But she could train the dog and take it to him anyway. Getting him to accept it might be difficult but the thought of doing something for him filled her with pleasure. Analyzing where that emotion came from would take too much energy and she pushed the thought aside. There would be time enough after he'd gone.

She frowned. Thinking about him being gone made her heart squeeze. The last conversations they'd had had been truly enjoyable. Other than her brothers, no one had ever teased her the way Mark had. She knew she was going to miss him after he'd gone.

"Angel?"

She glanced up with a start. "I'm sorry, did you say something?"

"Kind of went off into your own little world there, didn't you?"

A fire licked up into her face, and she dropped her eyes from his. "I'm sorry. I was just thinking."

"Did you lose a dog of yours?"

Confusion knitted her brows as she looked up. "What?"

"We were talking about dogs when you went off into la la land. I thought maybe you'd lost one."

"Oh. No, I'm like you, I guess. I spend so much time with the horses that I've never gotten a dog for myself. Paul was always the one with dogs. There were always three or four running around the place when he lived here. Now they're all with him at his new house. If I feel like I'm missing one, I just go to his house and romp around until the feeling goes away.''

Mark wanted to ask her why she'd been frowning, but he hated to push. Taking chances with their fragile relationship was too risky at this point. ''Angel?''

''Hmmm?'' She looked up when she realized what he'd called her. ''Why do you keep calling me that?''

He smiled. ''Does Jared have some sweatpants I could wear?''

A startled look sprang into her face, and he half expected her to stampede like a spooked herd of cattle. ''Why, are you cold?'' she asked.

A silly grin spread over his mouth as he watched her expression change yet again. ''No, but I would like to get up. The restroom, you know.''

''Oh.'' She managed to hide the heat in her face by jumping up and opening one of Jared's dresser drawers. She had her face under control by the time she lay a pair of gray sweats over the bed. ''I'll just take all this stuff out to the kitchen.'' She gathered his bowl and glass with the rest of the utensils she'd used for breakfast and hurried out of the room without looking at him again.

She took a few deep breaths as she deposited everything in the kitchen sink. She knew she should go back and make sure he was able to get up by himself, but she couldn't do it. Handling her attraction for him was much easier while he was lying in bed. Seeing all that bare skin while he was up on his feet would be too much. Which reminded her that she should have gotten him a shirt instead of just a pair of pants.

"Oh, for heaven's sake," she muttered out loud. "He's just a person like anyone else." She knew that should make her feel better but it didn't. He wasn't like anyone else because she'd never met anyone who could affect her the way he did. Once he left, she'd be able to forget him. However, until then she ought to do a better job of caring for him. His first time on his feet was no time for him to be alone.

With renewed determination she strode down the hall and made plenty of noise opening the door to Jared's room. She expected him to be in the bathroom with the door closed and was surprised to see him leaning heavily against the doorjamb with one of his hands holding his head.

"Mark?" She hurried over to him and grasped his arm. The shock of his smooth skin made her tingle, but it barely registered as she studied his face. "Mark, are you okay?"

"Just a little dizzy," he answered as he lifted his head. His eyes slowly cleared as he focused on her face. "It's going away now." He forced himself to smile as he noticed the look of worry on her face.

"Are you sure?"

"Yeah. I just moved too fast or something."

"Can you make it back to the bed?"

"Yeah." To prove it, he pushed away from the door and took halting steps in that direction.

She held on to his arm and after a few steps he leaned more of his weight on her. She could tell he wasn't feeling as well as he wanted her to think he was. She helped him sit down when they reached the bed and held his arm a little longer as she looked down into his face. His eyes were a little unfocused, and she watched until they began to clear.

The bruises around his eye seemed even more purple up close, and her eyes involuntarily wandered down his jaw where a dark stubble was already growing. The soft lighting highlighted the tawny skin of his upper body, and the color reminded her of a lion's hide. Her fingers itched to smooth across the varying shades until she remembered what she was doing. With a start her eyes darted back to his face.

He was watching her watch him, and she immediately pulled back. He caught her hand before she could withdraw completely and held it firmly while his other hand slipped between her hair and her neck. Sydney shivered noticeably, and he took a moment to caress the sensitive area from her jawline to her collarbone before gently pulling her back toward him.

The soft, light tug on her neck had her melting toward him. The faint touch of his lips against hers had her shivering again, but she resisted the urge to deepen the kiss. The sudden, intense desire she felt wasn't enough to make her forget the cut on his lip.

He seemed to be aware of it too as his feather-light touch drifted from her mouth down to her neck. His breath fanning against her skin was warm and intoxicating, making her tremble. He inhaled audibly as he leaned back. ''You're a beautiful angel, you know that?''

His voice sounded as heavy and thick as the desire pooling in her stomach. She couldn't respond as she met his gaze. He reached up to trace the outline of her lips, and her eyes dropped to his arm as she grasped the corded muscles of his wrist between her hands.

He sighed and closed his eyes, making her let go with a start. She jumped up and backed away. ''I'm sorry,'' she blurted as she backed farther away. She was sure she had hurt him, and she couldn't believe how selfish she'd been.

Mark's eyes snapped open and cleared immediately. He could see she regretted the contact with him. How stupid could he be to take advantage of the situation like that? The look in her eyes as she'd gazed at him had made him lose his head. After witnessing that violent episode out by the road it was no wonder she was pulling away. He didn't blame her—he just wished he knew how to get back on the easy footing they'd been on.

He offered her a small smile as he watched her back even farther away. "Don't be sorry, Angel."

His voice was soft and husky, and she wondered how much pain he was hiding. "Are you okay? I mean, now that you've eaten, maybe you could take something for the pain?"

"I'm all right," he said as his brows knitted together. What was she talking about? "I was just dizzy for a minute, but I'm fine now that I'm sitting down." She, on the other hand, looked like she could shatter at any second. "Are you okay?"

Sydney twisted her fingers together and clenched them until her knuckles began to ache. "Of course. I'm fine. I wasn't the one who was injured." Her voice sounded as stilted as her words, and she looked down at her sleeping bag to hide her confusion.

The sheets rustled as he slid back under the covers and leaned back against his pillows. "I guess we're both fine then. Which is a relief, let me tell ya."

Looking up with a nervous smile, she saw him gazing at her with a curious light in his eyes. Responding to his teasing was becoming second nature, and she smiled wider. "I'm sure. Since without me, you'd have a terrible time cooking anything for yourself.''

''That's certainly a major concern,'' he admitted. ''But I'll have you know with the proper equipment I can cook quite well.''

''What you mean is, you can boil water.'' She laughed at the look of outrage on his face and gladly slipped back into their easy camaraderie. Neither one of them seemed to want to address the meaning of the kiss they'd shared, and for now it was enough to pretend it hadn't happened.

''Boil water! Woman, I am mortally offended.''

She sat down on her makeshift bed as she tried not to laugh at his overexaggertion of outrage. ''I was too polite to tell you how offended I was when you wouldn't eat my toast.''

''I don't think toast is the proper word for what you concocted earlier this morning.''

She raised her eyebrows. ''You think you can do better?''

''I said, with the proper equipment. Electricity being a major necessity. I can prove it, you know.''

''Mmm-hmm. I'm sure.'' Her expression was the exact opposite of her words and the sarcasm wasn't lost on him.

He folded his arms across his chest. ''Them's fightin' words. You have just committed yourself to coming to my place for dinner after this storm releases us from this cozy little room.''

''I have?''

''Yes, you have. You have thrown down the gauntlet, and now you must enter the battle or pay the price.''

''What price?''

''I was afraid you were going to ask that.'' He stared up at the ceiling for a moment as if looking for divine intervention.

None was forthcoming, and he looked back at her with a smile. ''I can't think of one. Therefore, you have to come without argument.''

''There's a penalty for not naming a price,'' she stated matter-of-factly. This game was getting easier to play, and a warm glow spread throughout her system as she enjoyed it to the fullest.

''There is?''

''Yes. I'll come to dinner at your place and eat whatever you cook, but first you'll have to tell me why you keep calling me angel.''

''That's a stiff penalty,'' he answered as he made a face.

''We hicks from the sticks are known for our toughness.''

''So I've heard.'' He tapped his fingers against his jaw for a moment as he pretended to ponder her ultimatum. ''You'll eat whatever I cook?''

It was getting harder to keep a straight face, but she just managed it as she nodded.

He tapped his fingers some more. "You'll eat everything on your plate?"

A giggle escaped her before she clamped down on it. She nodded again.

With a huge sigh he gave in. His face settled into a serious expression, and with all teasing aside he answered her honestly. "When I first saw you, I thought you were an angel. A real one I mean. Well, you know."

She knew what he meant but couldn't believe what she was hearing. At the time she'd thought he believed her to be a kidnapper. And in reality he'd been thinking of her as an angel. The disbelief must have showed in her face for he went on.

"I was conscious part of the time while riding that horse of yours. I don't know—everything was a little fuzzy then, but when I first saw you I thought you had to be an angel. Because someone of your size couldn't possibly lift me over a horse. Anyway, the fuzziness went away, but you still saved my life. And you said that was the first time you'd ever gotten caught in a storm." He paused as he shrugged his shoulders. "Everything you've done for me reminds me of an angel. You saved my life, and I won't ever forget that."

Sydney couldn't hold his gaze and looked down at the floor. "I, um, don't know what to say."

"I just want to say thank you."

This time she was brave enough to look up.

"You're welcome. But no one could have seen what I saw and just walked away."

"Those punks walked away," he pointed out. "But the point is that you didn't."

Silence descended as she tried to come to terms with all that he had said. It was hard to adjust to, given all that she'd believed.

He could see she was reliving that moment, and he didn't want her to. "So, now you're committed to eating my cooking. You have no idea what a treat you're in for."

Chapter Six

The rest of the day passed quickly as they joked back and forth about nothing in general. The silliness of their conversations made a nice break from the seriousness of the storm outside and all that had happened since she'd heard the gunshots. Normally being cooped up inside was a hardship for Sydney, but she didn't even notice the passage of time as she shared a special closeness with a man she'd just met.

It felt as if she'd known him for most of her life. In their quieter moments she wondered how she could react so differently with this man. Making friends had always been difficult for her, but Mark had slid into her life as easily as she mounted a horse. It was easy to think that the stress had brought them together so quickly, and as soon as the storm was over their brief friendship would fizzle as well. She really didn't believe she'd ever have dinner at his place. As soon as he healed and got back to work, he'd forget all about her.

There would be so much work to keep her occupied after the storm that she wouldn't have time to see him anyway. She couldn't quite picture herself forgetting him, but given time the pleasant memories of their time together would fade. Thoughts like those made her sad, and with an effort she pushed them aside.

By nightfall Mark could no longer hide how exhausted he was. His five o'clock shadow was fast turning into a dark beard that accentuated the half-moon smudge under the one eye that wasn't bruised. He'd already shifted his pillows to allow him to lie flat on his back, and now it was all he could do to keep his eyes open.

He'd eaten almost an entire bowl of the canned stew she'd heated, and she was encouraged by his gradual recovery. "Why don't you try to get some sleep, Mark," she said as she walked over and extinguished the lantern beside the bed.

The shadows danced higher along the walls as a cloak of darkness descended over the room. The quilt on his bed took on an orangish cast from the reflection of the fire, and it was a strangely soothing contrast to the constant howling of the wind.

Mark's eyes fluttered as he tried to focus on her, but the heaviness of sleep won the battle. "I'm sorry. I'm not very good company," he half-mumbled.

"Ssshhh," she whispered as she watched his eyelids settle into a restful sleep. "You've been very good company." Her words were softly spoken, and he didn't even stir. She smiled as she watched him sleep. Having him with her had made braving the storm much easier, and it amazed her what a positive outcome had come of his tragedy. At least in her case. No doubt she would have been just fine on her own through this storm, but it had been nice to have company.

The events of the last thirty hours were catching up with her as well and a deep weariness had invaded her system. The stress was definitely taking its toll. Even though it was still early, she gave in to the need for more sleep. After a quick trip to her own bathroom upstairs, she returned to stretch out in her sleeping bag.

A strange sense of something being different snapped her eyes open as she strained to hear over the loud thrumming of her heart. The fire had died to a dull glow of embers, and she glanced quickly over her shoulder to check on Mark. His color was good, and after her panic subsided she was able to hear his steady breathing.

The zipper on her sleeping bag stuck, and she wrestled with it for a moment before giving up in exasperation and sliding out the narrow opening at the top instead. The rustle of the sheets on the bed as Mark moved in his sleep was the only noise she could hear as she threw another log on the fire.

The hiss of the flame as it caught the log seemed amplified, and she finally realized what had waked her. It was quiet. The windows had stopped rattling and the howl that had seeped through every crack in the house was gone. The wind had stopped.

Her watch steadily illuminated the time as twelve o'clock. She'd been asleep for about three hours. Her body wanted to crawl back under the covers, but she ignored her exhaustion as she tiptoed to the door and quietly went out into the hall. The cold air seeped up from the floor to encase her calves in its icy grasp before moving on to encompass the rest of her body. She hugged her arms around her chest as she moved to the front door and cautiously opened it.

Her eyes were adjusted to the dark since she'd left Jared's room without the flashlight, but even so, she couldn't see a thing. After giving her eyes time to get used to the deeper dark outside, she could make out hulking shapes on the front porch and out in the yard. The unevenness of the landscape confused her until she realized she was looking at snowdrifts. Huge ones. They were at least three feet tall in most places and probably higher in others.

The cold air had her quickly shutting the door as she hurried back to the fire. Pausing at Jared's door, she realized that now that the wind had stopped she could get out to check on her horses. The storm had blown itself out and more than likely the wind wouldn't start blowing again anytime soon. It would be safe to go outside even though it was dark. With a large camping flashlight she'd be able to see. It would be just as cold outside in the daylight as it was now.

Her mind made up, she eased the door open to retrieve her flashlight. She certainly wasn't going into the basement again in the dark. The floor creaked only slightly as she tiptoed to her bed. She was almost back out the door when Mark jerked awake.

"Sydney?" His voice was filled with a confused panic of being waked out of a deep sleep.

"I didn't mean to wake you. It's all right. Go back to sleep."

Propping himself up on one elbow to see her better, he asked, "Where are you going?"

"The storm's over. I'm going out to check on the horses."

"What?" He sounded wide awake now. "What time is it?"

"Midnight. Try to go back to sleep; you need

the rest.'' She turned and had her hand on the doorknob.

''You're going out in the middle of the night?''

''It's not going to get any warmer in the morning,'' she answered as she turned back to face him.

''The daylight would probably help though, wouldn't it?''

''I was just going to the basement for the big flashlight.'' The one she had in mind was shaped like a box and threw a beam almost as big as a car's headlight.

''Wait a minute.'' Exasperation and a tinge of panic colored his voice. ''That doesn't sound at all safe. What if the wind comes back up?''

''It's usually pretty calm right after a snowstorm. Don't worry, I'm not going to get lost. I'm really not going that far.''

''I'll come with you.'' He was already throwing the covers aside as he sat up.

''You will not,'' she answered sharply. She needn't have bothered to protest as she watched him wobble when a wave of dizziness hit him. She reached his side in one quick stride and laid her hand on his arm. ''Just sitting up makes you dizzy. I'm not going to be gone long. Why don't you try to go back to sleep?''

''I just got up too fast,'' he answered as he shook off her hand.

She crossed her arms as she stood over him to

keep him from standing up. "The drifts are waist-high at least. Just getting to the bathroom and back makes you tired. You are not going with me." She sighed and lowered her voice. "I don't know why you're so worried. I do this kind of thing all the time."

"You forget that I live in this area too. I happen to know that blizzards like this are not that common."

Sydney refused to budge. "I meant that I go out to check on my horses and feed them all the time. I do it in deep snow all winter long. The blizzard is over."

Mark had to lean back to see her face. "Couldn't you just wait till morning?"

"What's so magical about morning?"

"Your brother will be here, for one thing."

Sydney threw up her hands. "Of all the male chauvinist things to say. If you're worried about the wind coming up, it won't be any safer for Paul than it will be for me. I will have you know that I've been taking care of myself for a long time, and I'm going to continue doing so. You need to take care of yourself and stay in bed." She thrust her index finger at him for emphasis before she turned and headed for the door.

"Sydney!"

She ignored him and closed the door behind her. She had insulated coveralls in the closet by the front door as well as a heavy pair of snow boots. After getting the big flashlight from the basement she began pulling on her outerwear.

She was just stepping into her boots when Mark made it to the front door. He leaned against the door as he rubbed his arms for warmth. Jared's room was warm enough that she hadn't gotten him a shirt, and goosebumps dotted the skin of his bare upper body. The soft gray sweatpants rode low on his hips, accentuating the firmness of his stomach. The toes of his wool socks had slipped and the loose fabric flapped at the end of his feet.

Sydney straightened as she hefted the flashlight in one hand. "You're going to freeze to death out here."

"Do you really have to go, Angel?"

She caught her breath at the soft entreaty of his voice. Hardening her heart was an effort, but she just managed it as she answered. "I'm worried about my horses. I'll sleep much better after I've checked on them. There really isn't any danger, officer."

Mark jerked like he'd been slapped, and she almost relented. She knew she'd insulted him by being so formal with him, but responsibility to her livelihood won out.

"Nothing I could say is going to change your mind, is it?"

She clenched her teeth against the injury in his voice. "No."

He was beginning to shiver noticeably, and it took quite an effort for him to push away from the door. He turned his back on her and headed down the hall. She watched his hesitant steps until he made it to Jared's door. She swallowed against the constriction in her throat and then forcefully opened the front door and went outside.

Frosty air bit into the sensitive exposed skin on her face, and she sucked in her breath in reaction. The house had seemed icy, but it was much worse outside. She ducked her chin into her coveralls and plowed through the drifts to the barn. Snow had piled about two feet high in front of the doors, and she didn't bother to fight it.

Most of the drifts were hard enough from the wind to walk on, but occasionally she fell through and had to stumble her way out. She was panting from the exertion by the time she reached the fence. She paused to catch her breath and turned her flashlight into the corral on the south side of the barn. The ground had been swept clean on this side by the wind, and she climbed over the fence and entered the barn through one of the stall doors.

The sound of straw rustling reached her ears as the creak of the door spooked Blaze into motion. She turned her beam on the startled horse as she crooned, "Hey, boy. How you doin,' big fella?"

Blaze snorted and bobbed his head for an answer, and Sydney laughed in relief. It eased her mind considerably to see him on his feet with plenty of energy to spare. She hadn't liked leaving him wet and cold, but she hadn't had any choice.

The big black stretched his neck over his stall door and nudged her with his nose as if to reproach her for leaving him alone for so long. She ran her hand down his neck, taking note that his hair was dry and soft. ''You're probably hungry, aren't you, boy?''

Blaze nudged her again and the push was hard enough to send her back a step. She laughed again and turned to scoop up some grain. She poured the mixture of corn, oats, and molasses over his stall door into a small bin hanging there. As soon as he started to eat she went inside. After latching the door shut behind her she slid her hand under his blanket to reassure herself that all of him was dry. Thankfully he was, and she moved her hands down each of his legs, checking for injuries. He was perfectly fine, and she inspected his water and filled his hay net before leaving him alone.

The rest of the horses were west of the barn in a large fenced-in pasture. She had expected to get back before the storm hit and get them all in the corral, but she hadn't made it that far. The pasture was equipped with an open barn that had three sides and opened to the south. More than likely the horses were holed up there, and she headed that way through the drifts in the corral.

The beam of her flashlight lit the way as she stepped softly, falling through the drifts every now and then. Her heavy outerwear made it even more difficult to move through the snow, and she was panting by the time she reached the east side of the three-sided barn. "Hey guys." She greeted the horses as she walked around the side of the barn and turned her beam inside.

Some of the horses spooked and jostled around for a moment before turning startled eyes her way. "It's just me," she crooned as she turned the beam on herself. "Are you all in here?"

Talking to them as if they'd answer was second nature as she treated all of her animals as if they were human. The snorts and stomps she got were all the answer she expected. She didn't want to move through them in the dark and take the chance of being stepped on, so she contented herself with standing beside the wall and taking a head count. As far as she could tell they were all there. They were standing so close together it was hard to know for sure. "I hope you guys are all here. I'll go get you some grain—you wait here now."

She knew they weren't going anywhere but talking to them was an outlet she had always needed. Carrying a bale of hay would be too difficult through the drifts, but she could throw a bag of grain over her shoulder and make it okay.

Relief at finding her horses, coupled with the

cold air, had revived her sluggish muscles, and she turned back with renewed energy. Just before she climbed over the corral fence, the edge of her light caught a movement. She knew there weren't any animals in the corral, and she lifted her flashlight higher as her heart began to pound.

The hulking shape was moving toward her. Before true panic could set in she recognized Mark making his way around the biggest drifts in the corral. A tiny circle of light illuminated his feet from the flashlight in his hand.

''What are you doing?'' She didn't wait for an answer as she climbed the fence and plowed through the snow. Clouds of mist were billowing from her mouth like smoke signals by the time she reached his side. ''Are you nuts?'' It was hard to catch her breath after the huge burst of energy she'd just expended, but she managed to get the entire sentence out in one breath.

He was breathing hard as well, making a harsh sound in the still night air. ''Are you okay?''

Her anger drained away as quickly as it had come. His face was pale but set with a determination that no one could oppose. He was wearing Jared's coveralls and snow boots with a stocking cap on his head and heavy gloves on his hands. The ordeal of getting dressed should have worn him out, and her heart melted at the effort he had made for her.

"Yes, I'm fine," she said more softly as she caught her breath. "Come on." She grasped his arm and turned him toward the barn as her larger light shown the way.

He managed to keep pace with her all the way into the barn and over to a straw bale sitting in front of a stall. She sat down and pulled him down with her. "You're crazy," she said as she waited for his breathing to ease.

"You're the crazy one," he answered when he could talk.

No one had ever shown such concern for her before. Her brothers had always expected her to keep up with them, and her parents had raised her to be self-sufficient. Having someone worry about her to his own detriment was a new experience. "I can't believe you came out here."

"I can't believe you did either." He leaned his hands on his knees as he fought to steady his breathing.

"You're nuts."

He shook his head. "So are you."

"If we're going to argue, the least you could do would be to think up your own insults," she said as she leaned her head back against the wall.

"I'm conserving energy."

They had set both of their flashlights on the floor, but enough light pooled for her to see him sitting beside her with his shoulders slumped and his head tipped forward. "Are you going to make it?"

He turned toward her, but she couldn't see well enough to make out his expression. "I think I've told you how fine I am at least a hundred times."

"Oh, you're one to talk. Who was worried enough to come all the way out here after me? You're the one with the concussion, you know." She'd meant to sound outraged, but her voice came out soft with a definite note of caring in it.

"After all the times you've asked me how I am, I figured I was entitled to ask the same thing at least once."

"You couldn't wait until I got back inside?"

"Obviously not."

"I don't understand you," she said as she leaned back again and closed her eyes.

"That makes two of us."

That perked her attention. Opening her eyes, she noticed he was turned toward her and leaning closer. "What do you mean?"

He didn't bother to answer as he leaned even closer. It was too dark to make out his face, but Sydney knew he was going to kiss her. She responded by instinct and met him halfway. His lips were soft and searching, causing an eruption of reaction within her. A fire began pooling in her stomach, and she melted into him without a care for anything else. Neither of them thought about the cut in his lip as the kiss deepened.

Their bulky clothing kept most of their bodies apart, but somehow the lack of touch just enhanced the feeling of the kiss. The rough rasp of his glove caught in her hair, but she didn't even notice as she concentrated on how he was making her feel. Her limbs were heavy and weightless at the same time as she gave everything in her and received all that he had to give. A deep emotion pooled and leaped between them until finally they broke apart.

It was hard to breathe as her heart continued to pound, and she trailed her lips down his cheek to his neck. This time when he groaned she didn't pull back as his arms clutched her tightly to his chest.

"You're enough to drive a sane man crazy," he whispered in her ear.

"That doesn't sound like a compliment." Her words were muffled against his neck, and she pulled back enough to look at him.

With a sharp tug his right glove came off, and he slid his hand up to caress her cheek. His fingers slipped across her lips until his mouth followed with renewed fervor. It was the need for more air that made him lift his lips some time later. "Don't ever scare me like that again."

His breath fanned across her face from the whispered words. The sentence was punctuated with relief, making the order not very forceful. "And you tell me I worry too much," Sydney answered in a shaky voice. She was still too stunned by her reactions to think of anything original to say.

Mark lifted his chin and rested it on top of her head as he pulled her down to his chest. "Are you done out here now?"

She shook her head, loving the solid feeling of him underneath her cheek.

"You're not? Is something wrong?"

"No." She snuggled closer. "I was just going to take some grain to the horses in the pasture."

He didn't want to let go and reflexively squeezed her tighter. "How much grain?"

"A bag."

His sigh sounded heavy with resignation. "How are you going to do that?"

She pulled back and looked up into his face. It was too dark to make out his features, but she knew he was looking at her. "I was going to carry it. Why, do you have a better idea?"

"How much does a bag weigh?"

"There are fifteen horses out there. A fifty-pound bag isn't too much feed. That's only a little over three pounds per horse. They'll still be hungry, but it ought to tide them over until I can get them in the corral and feed some hay."

"You're planning to carry a fifty pound bag through those drifts all by yourself?"

Sydney stood up. The closeness they had shared had shattered like a broken mirror. He was treating her like a wimp who couldn't fend off a common horsefly. Obviously he had some mistaken notion that Jared and Paul did all the heavy work. It wouldn't surprise her to find out he really thought she was just the housekeeper.

She couldn't deny he was an attractive man or that he stirred her like no one else ever had, but he wasn't the man for her. He didn't even trust her to take care of herself. She'd be stupid to fall in love with a man like that.

Something painful lodged in her throat at that thought, and she blindly turned away. She grabbed her flashlight and marched to the back of the barn where she stored her grain.

''Sydney?''

She ignored the soft question in his voice while she hefted a bag over her shoulder. He was standing by the stall door with his light trained on her when she came back.

''Let me help,'' he said as he took a step toward her.

She brushed past him, blinded by a hurt and anger she couldn't control. ''I've got it, thanks.''

Her voice was cold and hard, and Mark frowned in surprise. He watched her move across the yard, the weight of the grain bag slowing her down and causing her to sway slightly. He realized he wouldn't have been much help, but her tone of voice was puzzling. Cursing the draining weakness in his body, he stayed where he was and waited for her to come back. He'd never felt so helpless in his life.

Even back on the road when he'd been fighting for his life, he hadn't felt this way. At least then he'd been struggling. The odds had been against him, and he'd known he wasn't going to win, but he'd never once felt helpless. Mostly he'd been angry. He'd made a snap judgment that had been wrong. So wrong that he would have paid for it with his life if it hadn't been for her.

He'd never met a stronger woman and he knew it wasn't just a physical strength she possessed. Ranching had to develop a determination and resistance most people never imagined, but he smiled to himself as he remembered her confession of hating to stay home alone. Maybe he wasn't totally helpless. At least he'd been able to contribute his presence and keep her company.

He'd enjoyed his time with her so much, he'd forgotten all about his father worrying about him or the stupid mistake he'd made on the road. His attention had been consumed with her, and he didn't see that going away just because he had to leave in the morning. He glanced up at the dark sky where not even one star was able to shine and wished it would start snowing again.

''Are you still out here?''

The voice startled him, and he practically jumped as he looked back down. He hadn't seen her making her way back. "Whoa, that was fast."

"I guess I'm stronger than you thought." The hurt in her voice was unmistakable and she winced at the sound. She hurried on to cover up, "Come on. Let's get inside before we freeze to death."

He'd said something to upset her but couldn't remember what it was. All he remembered was the soft feel of her lips under his and the sweet way she'd responded to him. The words they'd spoken after that were a blur. He moved off beside her as she turned toward the house, and he searched his mind for an answer.

Getting back through the snow was almost harder than getting out had been, and it took all of his concentration to stay on his feet. By the time they made it back, he was so tired he couldn't think about anything. He leaned against the wall to catch his breath once they made it inside.

Sydney stripped off her outerwear and stepped into her slippers. Mark hadn't moved except to gasp for breath, and she looked up in concern. "Are you okay?"

When he didn't move or answer, she went to his side. With shaking fingers she unzipped the coveralls and pulled them off his shoulders. He made an effort to help by shrugging them down but was too exhausted to do any more. "Lean on me," she commanded as she braced herself and tried to pull off one of his boots. It was awkward, but finally she managed to get the heavy clothing off without knocking him down. She was afraid if he fell down she'd never get him back to the warmth of the fire.

His breathing had eased somewhat, but it was obvious his energy was gone. Grasping his arm firmly, she guided him down the hall. She took it slowly and accepted most of his weight until they finally made it to the bed.

He collapsed back onto his pillows, and she pulled the covers over him. "Thanks," he managed to gasp, but his eyes stayed closed as if it were too much effort to even lift his eyelids.

"Get some rest," she whispered as she smoothed the comforter over his shoulders. Coming after her had been a crazy thing for him to do, and she hoped he wouldn't have any lasting repercussions from it.

She felt guilty for causing him to worry like he had. Concern flooded through her and wiped out the hurt and anger that had consumed her. They still had no electricity or phone service, and it was her responsibility to make sure he was all right. She'd gotten him through the storm but now was no time to be falling down on the job. He was still a long way from a hospital. Hopefully a good long sleep would revive him.

His face had lost some of its color and his breathing was more shallow than before. She retreated to her sleeping bag but was too uneasy and worried to sleep as her eyes never left his face.

Chapter Seven

An insistent buzzing like the sound of a pesky
fly made Sydney pull her arm out of her sleeping
bag to brush it away. The sound continued, even
got louder, and she swatted harder. Eventually it
dawned on her that she wasn't making contact with
anything and her arm was cold. How could her arm
be cold? Flies were only a pain in the summer
when it was hot.

She sat up as memory came rushing back. A
quick glance at Mark reassured her as she noticed
his color had come back, and he was breathing
deeper than she remembered. She must have fallen
asleep. She didn't remember crawling into her
sleeping bag, but obviously she had.

The fire had died again. The room was lit with

early morning light, but she was still sleepy enough to want to lie back down. The warmth of her bag was cozy, and she hated to have to get up to add a log to the fire.

Enticed by the thought of more sleep, she almost lay back down when she realized the buzzing noise had grown a lot louder. It hadn't been part of a dream. The last fuzziness of sleep left her when she realized she was hearing the engine of a snow-mobile. It had to be Paul.

Knowing how worried he must be to come out so early galvanized her into action. Not bothering with the zipper on her bag, she slid out and hurried to the front door. Putting on coveralls would take too long, so she settled for stepping into her snow boots and sliding into her jean jacket. Then she was out the door and bounding down the steps to greet her brother.

The bulky insulated coveralls Paul was wearing made him appear stockier than he actually was. Even as a boy he'd been thick chested, but now at the age of twenty-nine he was all chiseled muscle. A full chest and rippling biceps made his medium-sized frame appear quite stocky even without the added bulk of heavy clothes.

Cutting the engine with a quick move, Paul lifted his goggles and grinned at her. The exposed skin on his face was red and chapped from the cold, but he didn't seem to notice the discomfort.

"Sydney," he said, making her name sound like a word of relief.

"Yes, I'm fine," Syndey answered with a laugh. "How about you and Shannon and Kolt?"

Paul stood up and swung his leg over the powerful black machine. "They're still sleeping. Kolt's been having a great time. He thinks it's been an adventure that Mother Nature invented just for him." He shook his head at the exuberance of a two-year-old.

Sydney wasn't fooled. Kolt's antics were the subject of many a family discussion, and Paul loved to relate the joys of parenting to his single brother and sister. Sydney loved her nephew but as yet had no desire to experience a lively child firsthand.

Paul threw his arm around Sydney's shoulders as they turned and entered the house. "You sure you're okay?" he asked before letting go. "You look tired."

Sydney rubbed her eyes with one hand. "I am tired. You'll never believe what happened."

Paul tensed at the sound of her voice. "What?"

Sydney stepped out from under his arm. "Take off your coats and stuff, and I'll tell you. It's not that bad," she reassured him as she noticed the concern in his soft brown eyes.

The story she told him stilled his hands, and he was still standing in his coveralls by the time she finished. Sydney was shivering from standing around in her sweatpants, and she took off her own jacket with shaking fingers.

Paul watched her for a moment and in a few seconds stripped down to his jeans and socks before wrapping her in his arms.

''What's this for?'' She asked as she luxuriated in the heat pouring from his body.

''Are you sure you're okay, Sydney?'' The story she had told horrified him. He couldn't believe his sister had been dealing with such violence while he and his family had been actually enjoying the storm. They'd treated it like a camping trip to keep Kolt from being scared, and the only thing that had marred his own enjoyment had been his worry about Sydney. And now he found out he'd been right to worry.

''Don't be silly,'' she answered as she pushed out of his embrace. ''Of course I'm all right. Let's go in by the fire. I'm freezing out here.''

Paul followed right behind her as she led the way to Jared's room. She'd forgotten to close the bedroom door in her haste to greet Paul and was surprised to see Mark up and mostly dressed in his uniform when she stepped through the opening. She'd laid his clothes over a chair by the fire, and they appeared to be dry. Enough so that Mark was back in his tan pants and was buttoning his light blue shirt when they walked in.

"Oh, you're up already," Sydney said in surprise. Obviously he'd been wakened by their voices in the hall. She introduced her brother to him and watched as Paul strode across the room and shook hands with him.

Mark stood up to meet him, and Sydney was struck by the similarity in their height. Paul's size made him seem so much taller, but it was only that he outweighed Mark by a good forty pounds.

Mark wasn't sure of his welcome as guilt attacked him anew. If it weren't for his mistake, Sydney wouldn't have witnessed what she had. He was surprised when Paul greeted him with a smile.

"Good thing Sydney was out there," Paul said as he let go of Mark's hand. "You look like you took a good one."

Mark rubbed his fingers across his bruised cheek self-consciously. "Yeah. If it weren't for your sister, I would have paid for that mistake with my life."

Paul looked at Sydney in confusion. Sydney rushed to explain, "He's under the mistaken conclusion that what happened is his fault. I told him those three were intent on attacking him no matter what he did, but he hasn't listened to me."

Paul nodded like that made perfect sense. "Looks like you got bandaged up all right," he said as he ignored the issue of whose fault it was. "Sydney practices that kind of thing a lot on those horses of hers. Good thing you broadened her horizons a little bit. She and Jared never do anything but work.''

That was the last thing Mark had expected to hear, and he couldn't think of a thing to say.

''Hey, you'd probably like to get in touch with the cops,'' Paul said as he suddenly realized he had his cellular phone with him. ''Here you go.'' He handed it over and watched as Mark began to dial. ''Sydney, you surely haven't been keeping the room this cold all this time, have you?''

Sydney jumped. ''Oh. No. Of course not.'' She hurried over and put a couple of logs on the fire, and poked it until it flamed into life.

Paul sat down in the chair by the fireplace and extended his feet toward the warmth creeping out from the fire. ''Ah, that's much better.'' He rubbed his face to help it warm up as well before leaning closer to Syndey. ''He well enough to ride a snowmobile?'' he whispered.

She glanced over her shoulder to see Mark sitting on the bed talking quietly into the phone. She looked back. ''Yes, I think so. There's no other way to get him to the road today.''

''You're right about that. Some of those drifts are head-high. I think we got over a foot.''

''That much? I went out last night, but the only drifts I saw were about three feet high. It was about six inches deep everywhere else.''

"You checked on the horses?"

Sydney nodded. "Did you see the cattle on your way over here?"

"Most of them, I think. We need to get some hay out there this morning."

"I know," Sydney answered.

"Sydney?" Mark interrupted.

She turned toward him.

"Can a four-wheel drive make it back here?"

Paul answered for her with a shake of his head. "No way, man. If they've got the roads plowed, we can get you to the highway on a snowmobile, though."

Mark repeated that information and then looked up again. "How long will it take to get to the highway?"

"Fifteen minutes or so," Sydney answered.

After a few more minutes Mark handed the phone back to Paul. "The state patrol said they could be here in a half hour to an hour. Is that okay?"

"It's fine," Sydney answered as she stood up. "I'll go get some warmer clothes on and take you out there."

Before she got halfway to the door, Paul stopped her. "I'll go get your snowmobile warmed up. I'll start blading the roads out to the cattle while you're gone. When you get back we'll get the hay out there, okay?"

Sydney nodded. "I'll be right back, Mark."

"Hey, nice to meet you, Mark. Take care of yourself," Paul added as he crossed the room to shake hands again.

A thought occurred to Sydney, and she turned back. "Paul, have you called Jared to see when he can get home?"

"Talked to him this morning," he answered as he turned to face his sister. "I'm going to call him back here in a minute to tell them you're okay. He didn't know when the airport would open. It should be sometime today, though. Flying will probably be the easy part. Getting to the airport will be the tricky thing."

"Maybe I can help," Mark put in.

Sydney and Paul turned to him with the same question in their eyes.

"I can get him from the airport to your road, if you want to be there with a snowmobile."

"Oh, thanks, Mark. We appreciate the offer, but I don't think you should be driving." Her words sounded stilted to her own ears, and a stab of pain pierced her heart at the loss of the easy camaraderie they'd shared.

"My father can drive then. Have you got some paper? I'll write down my Dad's cellular number and my home number, and you can call me when you know Jared will be here."

"That's an awful lot of trouble to put you to,"

Paul said when he noticed the strain between the officer and his sister. He was beginning to wonder what had happened in the two days since the storm started.

''Saving my life was an awful lot of trouble for your sister too, but it didn't stop her. I'd like to help if I can.''

Paul smiled and nodded. ''We appreciate it.'' He pulled out a small notebook from his back pocket and a pen from the pocket in his shirt and handed them both to Mark.

Sydney chewed on her lip as she watched Mark write down his phone numbers. Tears sprang to her eyes at the gesture he was making for her. She blinked rapidly and hurried out the door before either of the men could see her emotional state.

That he would want to help and repay her somehow was natural enough, so why was she getting so teary eyed over it? After today, she'd probably never see him again. Another shaft of pain as quick and fierce as lightning stabbed through her chest at that thought. Caring for him and helping out naturally had made her care about him but surely not enough to make her cry when he left. Except it was all she could do not to cry.

She'd like to blame that on being overtired, but she knew she couldn't. Repaying her by helping out was nice of him, but she knew it was just a duty to him. Responsibility alone would be enough to drive him to cancel out the debt he thought he owed her. It wasn't anything more on his part, and she knew that's where her tears were coming from.

She wanted to be more than a responsibility or a duty. A lot more. Now that she was forced to face his leaving, she realized her feelings were deep where he was concerned. So deep that she'd fallen in love with him.

What a stupid thing to do. Not only had she given her heart away to a man who wouldn't remember her a year later, but she'd fallen in love with a police officer. A man who had one of the most dangerous jobs imaginable. Somehow none of that mattered. She loved him for who he was. What he did and where he went made no difference. The choice had been taken away from her the first time she'd spoken to him.

With a heavy heart she walked back downstairs. She'd changed into long johns underneath a pair of blue jeans and had just left on the two sweatshirts she was already wearing.

Mark was waiting for her by the front door. He was fully dressed in his uniform with his heavy navy jacket zipped to his neck. ''You should wear Jared's coveralls and boots, Mark. If you're going to pick him up at the airport, he can wear them back.''

''I might wear his stocking cap,'' Mark answered. ''The rest you can have waiting for him on his snowmobile.''

"You'll be cold."

Mark shook his head. "It's not that far."

Sydney's emotions were too raw to argue, and she handed him a hat while she stepped into her own coveralls and boots. Paul had her machine warmed and ready to go, and after Mark slid on behind her she shifted into gear and took off down the lane.

The pressure of his thighs against her own made a little tingle slide down her spine. This would be the last time she would ever touch him, and she couldn't help but luxuriate in the feeling. The rush of cold air against her face from the speed of her snowmobile didn't even register as she noticed the solidness of his chest against her back.

She drove at an even speed across the unevenness of the drifts. In places the land was swept clean by the wind and in others the drifts were four to six feet tall. There wasn't a cloud in the sky, but the sun was so far away that it did little to warm the air. Sunlight glittered off the hard, stark whiteness all around, and she realized too late that she'd left her tinted goggles in the house. Her eyes narrowed to tiny slits to shut out the glare, but even that wasn't enough to dampen her awareness of the man behind her.

All too quickly they reached the road, and she switched off the machine. A sort of stillness settled over them as the sound of the machine died away.

There wasn't a car in sight in either direction, and the winter wonderland scene in front of them was soothing and peaceful.

"If it wasn't for you, I'd be buried under all that snow right now."

Sydney jerked around at his tone of voice and followed his gaze to the side of the highway. "Well, you're not buried under all that snow. You can't help what happened now. There's no sense in imagining what could have been. It didn't happen and you're going to be okay. That's all that matters." Her voice was sharper than she'd intended, but she couldn't help it. His words had frightened her. She couldn't imagine not having him in this world somewhere. Maybe it wasn't meant to be for her to have him, but at least she could know he was alive. And she'd never regret the last two days she'd had with him.

"I didn't mean to sound like I was borrowing trouble. I meant to say thank you—for everything."

"Oh well, you're welcome. Thanks for offering to bring Jared home."

"It's the least I could do, Angel."

Sydney shifted sideways so she could make eye contact. "I'm no angel, Mark. I'm sure I'm no different from anyone else."

He pulled his hand out of his pocket and lightly stroked her cheek. "I don't think there's another woman alive like you, Angel."

She wished she knew what he meant by that. Did he really care that much or was he just saying thank you? She wanted to ask but didn't dare. His blue eyes so close to her own were filled with emotion, but she couldn't read what it was.

The rumbling of an engine drifted to her ears as she watched his eyes dip closer. Her own eyes floated closed as their lips met. Mark slid his hand to the back of her neck as the kiss deepened. Instinctively she pressed closer. Knowing that he was only thanking her couldn't dim the passion flooding her own veins.

If it wasn't for the roar of the nearing engines, she would have lost all track of time and space. As it was, Mark pulled back long before she was ready to lose contact with him. Her feelings showed plainly in her eyes as she gazed up at him and for this moment she didn't care. If he didn't know how she felt, she'd never have a chance with him. Letting him see everything was her only hope.

His eyes roamed freely over her face as if memorizing every detail. An orange dump truck with a huge blade on the front pulled up beside them. Two state patrol cars followed behind. A man a little taller and heavier than Mark jumped out of the first police car. "Mark!"

Mark glanced up quickly and then looked back down.

''God, Mark.'' The man was running toward them as fast as he could through the snow.

Taking the time for another quick kiss, Mark stood up. He shifted his attention to the man, and Sydney watched as he walked away. The man grabbed him in a bear hug, laughing and crying at the same time. It seemed odd at first that he should be crying, until it dawned on her that this man looked a lot like Mark. Their builds were the same, and they had similar eyebrows and noses. The older man had gray hair at his temples, and she knew he had to be Mark's father.

Tears pooled in her eyes as she realized that Mark's homecoming with his father was her loss. He was going back to his life now and her time with him was at an end. She didn't want Mark to see her cry, so she fired up her snowmobile and spun around before Mark left his father's embrace.

Chapter Eight

"Who was that, Mark?" Kent Adams asked as he stepped back from his son.

With a heavy sigh Mark watched her disappear over the rise. "That was an angel, Dad."

Kent stepped in front of his son and took a closer look at his eyes. The glare of the sun made it impossible to tell if his pupils were normal or not. "Care to explain that?"

Another sigh escaped him as he turned his gaze on his father. "She saved my life. Can you believe she was strong enough to throw me over a horse?"

Kent looked back at the trail left by the snowmobile. "Sounds like a good story," he said as he pulled on Mark's arm and led him toward the waiting patrol car. "Why don't you tell me about it on the way to the hospital."

"I don't have time for that," Mark answered as he followed along to the car. "We're picking her brother up from the airport sometime today." He glanced at his father's hip to make sure his cellular phone was there and breathed a sigh of relief when he saw it was.

"They haven't opened the airport yet," Kent answered as he opened the rear door and held on to it with one hand. He stood silently by while Mark greeted the other two state patrolmen. The immense relief they all felt at finding Mark alive was evident in the emotional welcome he received from his fellow officers.

Tears were shining in everyone's eyes by the time the cold chased them inside the automobiles. Getting all three vehicles turned around on the icy road was a slow process, but eventually the snow-plow led the way back to town.

Tears were blurring Sydney's vision as she fought to control her snowmobile. The glare of the sun was much worse on her wet eyes, and she could barely see where she was going. She couldn't afford to let Paul see her in this state and stopped to dry her eyes.

Taking several deep breaths helped to calm her, and the knot in her throat slowly loosened. There was too much work to do to waste time sitting around bawling. With a quick shake of her head she choked down her feelings and shifted her snowmobile into gear.

Battling the elements took over, and the rest of the day went quickly as she and Paul struggled to get hay to the cattle. Feeding the horses was much easier. All she had to do was open the corral gate and herd the horses in with her snowmobile. Dumping hay and grain into the feedbunk along one side of the corral was nothing more than a necessary chore—one she performed twice a day every day of the year.

The horses were frisky and playful as they ran around the enclosure and plowed through or jumped over the drifts inside. Sydney even managed to laugh at their antics.

Paul came up behind her as she stood watching the horses. "Well, the airport finally opened. Jared's catching a flight that lands at five-thirty. You want to call Mark and relay the information?"

Sydney's face paled at the thought. She didn't think she was capable of talking to him again, knowing what she did. There were probably women capable of talking to a man they were in love with and couldn't have, but she wasn't one of them. "Why don't you go ahead? I was just going in to heat us some tea."

"What happened between you two?" Paul asked as his brows narrowed in concern.

Sydney started and jerked her gaze to his face. "What do you mean?"

"Things seemed rather tense between you two earlier this morning, and now you don't want to talk to him. What did he do? You're not hurt, are you?"

She'd never felt so hurt in her life, but she knew that wasn't what her brother was asking. "Of course I'm not hurt. And he didn't do anything. He had a concussion, for crying out loud."

Paul shifted and closed the distance between them. "All right. So why the tension?"

All the feelings she'd forced back surged forward again, and she spun away to hide the tears in her eyes.

Paul laid his hands on her shoulders. "Sydney?"

She took a deep breath and wiped her eyes. She wasn't going to cry. She wasn't. "It's nothing." Her voice cracked and she cleared her throat. "I'd just rather you talked to him, that's all."

In all the years he'd spent with his sister, he had never seen her cry over another human being who wasn't family. She'd cried when a kitten had accidentally been run over and Jared had to bury it. And tears had wet her face the first time he'd sold one of his dogs and the first time she'd sold one of her horses, but never over someone who wasn't family. "It's not nothing if you're crying over it,

Sydney. He seemed nice enough to me. Was he mean to you?''

A harsh laugh escaped her at that. ''No, he wasn't mean. He was actually quite wonderful. But he isn't coming back.''

Paul lifted his head as realization dawned. Well, what do you know? ''He is coming back. He's bringing Jared from the airport.''

''That's just a duty. He feels like he has to pay me back for helping him.''

Paul pondered that for a moment. ''All right, I'll call him. That tea sounds good by the way. The cold is starting to seep all the way to my bones.''

''I'll heat some water in Jared's room. I'm sure the fire's still going.'' Relief that Paul was going to help her fueled enough energy for her to charge toward the house. That she was running away with her tail tucked between her legs was something she wasn't willing to consider.

The emergency room was crowded and most of the day was gone by the time the doctors allowed Mark to leave. He was under strict orders to take it easy for at least a week while the effects of the concussion wore off. His father waited with him the entire time, and it wasn't until they were walking out of the hospital that Kent's cellular phone rang.

Kent answered it and handed it to Mark. ''It's for you.''

Mark's eyes lit up and then quickly dimmed as he realized he was talking to Paul and not Sydney. Paul was polite enough, asking after Mark's health and making sure he was capable of picking up Jared before giving him the flight number. There was a reserve in Paul's tone that hadn't been there earlier that morning and a niggle of worry insinuated itself into Mark's mind. "Is everything okay, Paul? Did Sydney get back all right?" Visions of her having an accident on her snowmobile flooded his mind.

Paul smiled at the worry in Mark's tone. It didn't sound to him like Sydney had her story straight. In his opinion it couldn't hurt to help out a little bit. "Physically she's fine. The crying bothered me though. Never seen her do that except over an animal or one of us."

"You said she was fine. What is she crying for?" Mark's voice raised in alarm. "Put her on— I want to speak to her."

"Uh, I can't put her on; she's in the house. I figured you could tell me why she's crying. As far as I can tell it has something to do with you."

This didn't make any sense, and Mark gripped the phone tighter in frustration. "What are you saying, Carrigan?"

"Oh, I think you know. The question is—what are you going to do about it?"

The message Paul was sending was loud and

clear, and Mark loosened his hold on the phone as a smile spread over his face. "I hadn't planned on moving that fast." He didn't want to give too much away to her brother. It wasn't any of his business after all. But Paul's words left a warm glow in his chest that hadn't been there before.

"Sometimes fate sets a fast pace. Bucking it can do more harm than good."

Mark raised his eyebrows at Paul's blunt manner. "I wouldn't think you would approve of a police officer for your sister. Especially after what happened." Kent's eyebrows raised at that, and Mark turned away from him.

"I get the impression that most police officers are honest, hardworking people. Are you saying you're not?"

"No. I'm saying it's a dangerous job."

There was a pause over the wire and then Paul came back forcefully. "Some people claim breaking horses is a dangerous job."

That point hit home like an arrow piercing the bull's-eye of a target. "I think you have a different view than most people." It was a weak effort at a defense but the best Mark could think of.

"Most people don't count. What Sydney thinks is all that should matter. You ever ask her opinion on that?"

"Well, no."

"I think you owe it to her to ask, and I'm not

talking about responsibility because she helped you when you needed it.''

''Does your whole family talk as plain as you?'' Mark asked as he tried to catch his breath. It felt as if Paul were stampeding him like a herd of cattle.

''We're honest folk.''

Mark had to laugh. Paul was trying to sound like a country bumpkin, but it wasn't enough to hide the steely sharpness of his personality. ''I hear you, Carrigan. I'll have your brother home as soon as I can.''

It wasn't the answer Paul wanted, but he had to admire Mark's determination. A man strong enough to stand up to him ought to be good enough for his sister. ''We appreciate it,'' he answered as he gave in a little bit.

''You're welcome,'' Mark answered before handing the phone back to his father.

Kent put the phone back in the leather case on his belt and looked up in time to catch a vacant look in his son's eyes. ''Care to tell me what that was all about?''

''Yeah, we better head to the airport if we're going to get there by five-thirty. It's going to be a lot of driving on bad roads. Are you sure you're up to it, Dad? I know it's been a long day for you too.''

''I had Roger drop off my Explorer earlier this

morning.'' He walked ahead out to the parking lot and spotted the Ford four-wheel drive one of the other officers had left for him. Without looking directly at his son, he tried again. ''There was more to that conversation than flight times.''

Mark missed a step in his stride before regaining his balance and hurrying to catch up. He didn't answer immediately, instead waiting until they both had climbed in the new black vehicle his father had bought just a month before. While his father shifted into gear and pulled out into traffic, Mark sat back and cleared his throat. ''I never expected to find a woman I'd want to marry. The job has always been more important to me, and I saw what it did to you and Mom. I've never wanted to put a woman through that.''

Kent glanced over in surprise. This was the first time he'd ever heard that. ''Is that what you think, son? That the job ruined my marriage?''

''I think it was a big part of it.'' He had never discussed it with his father before because he hadn't wanted to get in the middle of it. The personal things between his parents weren't any of his business. And now he looked out the window at the piled snow along the road to avoid his father's gaze.

''I imagine it seemed that way to you,'' Kent said almost to himself as he remembered how it had been. ''Being a police officer was just a symptom, Mark. The truth was your mother and I weren't happy with each other for quite some time. We grew apart in ways that had nothing to do with what I did for a living. I began spending more of my time and energy on work to escape the unhappiness at home. You and I have both heard about marriages that didn't make it because of the job, but it doesn't have to be that way for you. If you let the woman in your life know how important she is to you every day of your life, you'll overcome the problems that arise because of what you do.''

Mark turned to study his father. "I always thought Mom couldn't take the danger you lived with every day."

Kent met his eyes. "It was just a convenient way to strike out at me, saying that." Before Mark could interrupt he hurried on. "Don't get me wrong—I hit back at her in lots of ways myself. Like I said, we grew apart. I never meant for it to get as bitter as it did. We tried to hide that from you, but I know we didn't do a very good job. I'm sorry about that, son. Don't let my mistakes color your life."

Mark nodded as he finally understood more of what had happened between his parents. "It's still a lot to ask of any woman," he said as he looked back out the window.

"There's potential danger in everything, son.

Just getting in a car every day is a risk. It takes a strong person to do the job and a strong one to live with that person. Sounded to me like your lady is a strong one. Lifted you over a horse, didn't you say?''

Mark laughed. ''That's different.''

''Is it? Did she panic? Did she waste time in a blizzard to the point where she couldn't save either of you? Everything she did was on her own since you weren't conscious at the time. The story you told me sounded like she has strength. A lot of it.''

Mark glanced at his father in surprise and then turned to stare out the front window. He'd never thought of it that way. His own guilt at putting her through that experience had never let him look at it from her point of view. It had scared her; he'd seen that for himself, but she'd done what needed doing anyway. She'd even gotten angry when he'd told her she shouldn't have witnessed something that violent. At the time he'd felt so responsible that he hadn't paid much attention to her reaction. She'd been defending herself by getting angry with him.

Come to think of it, she'd tried to tell him several times how strong she was. He'd insulted her in the barn that last night. That was why she'd gotten angry and taken off with that bag of grain without letting him help. Her brother obviously knew the depths of her personality and had faith in her. Paul, in his blunt way, had said as much. His heart lifted as he realized that he was attributing characteristics to her that didn't exist. According to his father, they hadn't existed in his mother either.

Kent watched him mull everything over in his mind and inwardly sighed in relief when he saw Mark break into a smile. "Hey, I almost forgot to tell you," he said as Mark's mood shift reminded him of the reason behind the bruises on his son's face. Mark turned to him at the note of excitement in his voice. "They found your car. Those punks skidded off the interstate not far from Loveland and plowed through a fence before getting stuck in a huge drift. The entire incident, from when you stepped out of the car until they crashed, was captured on the videotape in your car. It shouldn't take long to ID them. They already ran the plates on the Mercedes. It was stolen—haven't found it yet, but we will."

Mark's face remained impassive at the news. "I thought it was a couple of rich kids out for a joyride in their daddy's car. The driver was dressed like any kid, and I made a snap judgment that could have cost me my life."

"According to the guys who reviewed the tape, you didn't have time to make any mistakes," Kent argued. "You had a decent distance between you when you took his license. He went from smiling to lunging at you in an instant. You know we're not trained to read minds. The kid was a good actor. He had just the proper amount of nervousness for getting stopped for speeding. The impression I got was the top brass is impressed with how well you fought them off. A man in worse physical condition than you wouldn't have made it.''

Mark shook his head. ''I should have been more wary of the kid—made him go sit in the car. He was such a skinny runt that I never thought to be threatened.''

''Exactly. You had no reason to feel threatened. You hadn't even looked at his license much less ran it through to know the car was stolen. Police are attacked all the time. You can't know when it's going to happen. What you can do is stay in shape to fight them off. Which you did. You did everything any officer could have. I'm grateful they didn't put a bullet in you, but I'm still going to see them go down for this. There won't be any plea-bargaining on this attempted murder charge.''

The anger in his father's voice brought home to Mark how much his Dad must have worried about him during those two nights of the storm. He reached over and gripped his father's shoulder. ''This was probably harder for you than it was for me. I'm sorry I couldn't get in touch with you, Dad.''

Kent placed his hand over Mark's and squeezed. ''You're alive, son. That's all that matters.'' They both blinked back tears as Kent turned his head toward the road. "I want to meet this guardian angel of yours. She's given me the greatest gift in this world. I know I don't say it enough." He glanced over at Mark with a wobbly grin. "I love you, son."

Mark swallowed hard against the knot rising in his throat. "I love you too, Dad."

Chapter Nine

Paul found Sydney tending the fire in Jared's room. The thick smell of vegetable soup permeated the room, and he sniffed in appreciation as his stomach rumbled. Her ponytail hung limply down her back as she bent over the fire turning the kettle of water. There was a tray full of sandwich-makings by her knees, and seeing that made him realize they still didn't have electricity. "Power still off, huh?" It was an obvious question, but it got her attention as she spun around in surprise.

"Oh, Paul, you scared me. I didn't hear you come in. No, there's no power and the phone still doesn't work either. I was just making us a late lunch. Are you hungry?" As soon as the last words left her mouth she realized how stupid they sounded. Paul was always hungry and could eat as much as several men combined.

''I could eat.'' They both smiled at the understatement.

She dished him a full plate and handed it to him as he sat down next to her on the floor. ''When do you think we should be out there to meet Jared?'' she asked.

''I doubt they'll make it here before eight-thirty or nine. I thought we'd just leave his snowmobile out there. We can put it on this side of the hill so no passing motorist can see it. Jared will probably call me before he gets here, and I'll tell him where it is. I'm kinda anxious to get home and see how Shannon is doing.''

Sydney nodded and restrained herself from asking how the conversation with Mark had gone. She half-expected Paul to volunteer the information, but he kept his discussion to the work they'd accomplished that day and what was left to do in the next few days.

After he stuffed himself with three sandwiches while she had barely nibbled on one, they headed out again to leave Jared's snowmobile by the road. Once that was done, Paul let her off back at the house. ''You gonna be okay?''

Sydney turned toward him at the sound of concern in his voice. She'd heard that note in his tone often when he was speaking to his wife or son, but rarely was she ever gifted with it. "Sure. Of course." She patted his arm and headed for the warmth of the fire.

"Sydney?"

She turned back.

"Give him a chance. It might not be as bad as you think it is."

She considered that for a moment. "Did he say something to make you think so?"

"Not exactly." He hurried on when he saw her face fall with disappointment. "I got the impression that what he's doing for Jared has nothing to do with duty or responsibility, though."

Before she could ask more, he revved his machine and took off. She stood looking after him for a long time until the cold seeped inside her muscles and grabbed her attention. Slowly clomping her way up the steps, she thought about hope. Paul had tried to instill it in her, but she wasn't sure it was such a good idea. If she sat around waiting for something to happen, it would hurt that much more when it didn't.

Her movements were slow and methodical as she undressed at the door and wandered down the hall to Jared's room. Sinking down on her sleeping bag, she wrapped her arms around herself and gazed at the flames. It was true that Mark had kissed her three times, but that didn't necessarily mean anything. As far as she knew, men didn't take kissing all that seriously. Some of them didn't even take making love all that seriously, so she knew she couldn't put much store into the kisses she'd shared with Mark.

He was probably just grateful. In his place, she would be too. His use of the term ''angel'' was puzzling, though. It had sounded like an endearment at the time, but it could be explained away as well. It kind of put her on a plane that was out of reach for a mere mortal. It wasn't quite the same as being put on a pedestal. No, it could be just another form of gratitude.

The trouble was she didn't have enough experience with men to know. The only men she knew well were her brothers, and they hardly counted. A sarcastic laugh escaped her as she realized she was probably the only twenty-five-year-old woman in the United States who could say she didn't have experience with men. Her life had always been so focused, so obsessed with horses that dating had never mattered.

She'd been tempted by a few men once she'd graduated from high school, but they'd never been that sincere, and she'd never had that much time. The interest just wasn't there and she'd never worried about it before. Now she wished she'd taken the time. Maybe then she'd have a clue about Mark.

The other guys she knew seemed pale in comparison with Mark. Even with bruises all over his face, Mark was twice as handsome as anyone she'd ever met. And he was so considerate, worrying about her out in the dark by herself. It had made her angry that night, but the emotion hadn't lasted. Who could stay angry in the face of such concern? It was obvious that Mark was different—special. He'd brought her heart out of solitary confinement without even trying.

And now that her heart was out, it was bursting. Love and pain were so intertwined within her that she could hardly stand it. That was why she didn't think hope was such a good thing. Hope made her heart grow bigger, and she was afraid she didn't have the room for it.

The roads were clear but still icy and snow-packed, slowing the traffic to a crawl near Denver International Airport. Even so, Jared and Kent made it on time to meet Sydney's brother. Signs of exhaustion were on all the faces exiting the gate, making it obvious how much of an ordeal it had been to get to Denver.

Mark looked twice at the rugged face under a black baseball cap. The man had an average build and black hair peeped out under the sides of his hat, but the eyes looked familiar. They were an older, more creased version of Sydney's.

Mark was still dressed in his uniform, and

Jared's eyes locked with his. He watched while Jared hefted a duffel bag higher on his shoulder and walked toward him. "Jared Carrigan?" Mark asked as he saw the question in the other man's eyes.

Jared smiled. "You must be the police officer my brother was telling me about." He held out his hand and gripped Mark's tightly.

"Mark Adams," he answered. When Jared let go of his hand he gestured toward his father. "This is my father, Kent. He got roped into doing the driving."

"Glad to meet you," Jared said as he shook hands with Kent. "I'm sorry to bring you two out on a night like this."

"I'm glad I finally get to meet one member of this family I've been hearing about," Kent put in. "It's no trouble at all to be here."

Jared looked back at Mark and took note of the swelling in his face. "Paul told me a little bit about what happened. I'm sure you'd rather be at home than out driving icy roads in the dark."

Mark led the way toward the trains that would take them back to the terminal. "It looks worse than it is. But if it wasn't for your sister, I wouldn't be here at all."

Jared studied him thoughtfully. "I'd like to hear about it."

Kent was only too happy to elaborate on the

story he knew secondhand. Mark was glad that he was telling it, saving him from glossing over the emotions and feelings he had for Sydney.

Jared didn't have any luggage other than the duffel bag he was carrying, and Kent was still telling the story as they climbed in the Explorer. Jared sat in back, throwing his duffel bag on the seat beside him.

"Now let me get this straight," Jared said as Kent finished repeating the tale. "Sydney brought you in on her horse because the storm was turning into a blizzard, is that right?"

Mark twisted in his seat to meet Jared's gaze. "That's right."

"And I'd like to know what she was doing out there when that storm had been forecast for days." He said it almost as if he were talking to himself.

Mark almost laughed as he realized Sydney had pegged her brother perfectly. "She said you wouldn't be happy about that. But if she hadn't been there, I wouldn't be here."

Kent glanced in his rearview mirror to get a look at Jared. "Whatever you feel about her being out there, let me tell you I'll never forget what she did for my son."

"I understand where you're coming from, but they both could have frozen to death out there," Jared responded with heat in his tone.

"In the larger scheme of things, 'could haves'

don't mean much,'' Mark said quietly. That was a lesson that had been brought home to him in spades. He'd been like Jared all along, thinking about his mistakes and all the things that could have happened. Now he could see that was a waste of time. Blaming himself was a waste of emotion and worrying about what could happen in his relationship with Sydney ten years down the road was just as wasted. What did matter was what had happened and what he could make happen.

''I didn't mean to make light of the fact that she saved your life.'' This time Jared's voice was soft with respect.

Mark smiled. ''She was so sure she could make you see how keeping that horse had been necessary. The horse was the only one that knew the direction to the house.''

''If you weren't sitting there alive and fairly healthy, I'd tell you how much more stupid that makes the whole thing.''

''She would have made it back with no problem if she hadn't stopped for me.''

''I'm sorry,'' Jared answered. ''You're right and I didn't mean to argue with you. When Paul told me what happened, I couldn't believe it. There I was in sunny Sun City, and there she was in the middle of a blizzard, fighting for her life. It didn't seem right, and I couldn't believe how much it scared me.''

"I know what you mean," Kent put in.

Mark tuned out as he realized what they were saying. He'd met three loved ones who'd been on the outside of a dangerous situation not able to do anything. Now that it was over, the jitters had set in on everybody. But it didn't make any of them walk out. The danger hadn't chased them away. Loving someone meant worry, pain, and relief when it was all over, but it didn't mean the relationship had to end.

Maybe there was a chance for him with Sydney after all.

The drive back seemed to take forever as Mark anticipated seeing Sydney again. He didn't have a good plan for what to say to her but figured he could improvise as he went. The highway was dark and deserted as Kent pulled to a stop next to the sign proclaiming THE CARRIGAN RANCH. The headlights illuminated the top of the small rise west of the road, making it obvious that no one was there.

Jared opened his door and stepped out. Mark and Kent followed, both pulling their jackets higher and tighter at the sudden blast of frigid air. The soft click of their doors shutting and the swish of their shoes on the snow were the only sounds. "I would have thought they'd be here by now," Mark said as he scanned the area around them.

Jared lunged through the nearest drift and worked his way to the top of the small hill that led to his house. Kent crossed his arms and shivered. ''I hope he's not planning to walk.'' He said this out of the side of his mouth in a quiet tone to keep Jared from hearing.

''I'm sure he's not,'' Mark answered. The darkness away from the vehicle was so midnight blue that Jared became a wavering black shadow as he labored through the snow.

''Here it is,'' Jared called down from the hill. ''They left my snowmobile out here for me.'' Setting his duffel bag on the ground, he stepped on his machine and brought it quickly to life. He gave it a chance to warm up as he walked away and called down again, ''Thanks for the ride. I'm just going to go on from here.''

That made sense to Mark since he wouldn't have wanted to walk through those drifts twice either. Disappointment engulfed him as he realized he wouldn't be seeing Sydney after all. Jared's shadow grew taller as he lifted his arm to wave and Mark listlessly responded.

He would have continued to stand there if it wasn't for his father grabbing his arm. ''Let's get out of here. I'm freezing.''

Mark took one last look and then turned his back to climb in the Explorer. It was irrational to be so despondent; he knew he could call her at any time, but he'd been so sure he would see her again that night. The landscape he could see in the beam of the headlights suddenly looked hard, frozen, and barren.

The buzzing of an engine roused Sydney from her fascination with the fire, and she jumped to her feet in a wild dash to the front door. The last few hours by herself had brought home to her how lonely and isolated the ranch was, and she was eager for Jared to fill their home with his personality.

Watching from the door she saw him drive into the barn. After a moment, she could make out a shadow closing the barn door before moving toward the house. His shape grew larger until his face became clear in the beam of her flashlight. "You made it!" Her voice was high with excitement, and without a thought she catapulted herself into his arms.

Jared took a step back to brace himself. "Whoa, what's this for?"

Usually the most demonstrative sign of affection they shared was a good punch in the arm, making this hug of welcome seem out of place. "I missed you." An attack of self-consciousness invaded her, and she quickly stepped back. "And I was worried about you traveling in this weather."

Jared shut the door behind him and moved farther into the house. "Man, it's cold in here. Still no power, huh?"

"Nope. Come on," she said as she headed down

the hall. "I've got a good fire going in your room."

Jared followed her into his room and immediately noted the dishes by the fire, her crumpled sleeping bag, and his unmade bed. "Took over my room, did you?"

"I really couldn't carry the police officer up the steps to my room, you know. It seemed better to build just one fire since I didn't know how long we'd be without power."

Jared smiled at the defensiveness in her tone. "I didn't mean anything by it. I guess you've had it hard while I was gone. Those officers were sure impressed with you." Setting his bag on the floor, he crossed to the fire and warmed his hands.

"What do you mean?" Sydney asked as she sank onto her sleeping bag.

He glanced over his shoulder. "I guess they were both just really happy that Mark was alive. They said it was thanks to you."

Here it comes, she thought. Getting this issue out of the way would at least take her mind off other things. "You're probably hacked at me for being out there in the snow, aren't you?"

"Scared is more like it." That got her attention and she looked up at him. "When Paul told me what happened, I couldn't wait to get home to see how you were for myself. I'll tell you, this has been the longest day of my life."

"Didn't Paul tell you I was fine?"

"Of course, but I wanted to see for myself. I was all worked up to jump all over you for being out in that storm until Mark told me he'd be dead in that case. Even so, that was stupid, Sydney."

His words lacked conviction, and she smiled. She couldn't believe how easy she was getting off. "Blaze came in real handy. I was impressed with how well he responded to everything. It was a good decision keeping him." She knew she was pressing her luck with that one, but she couldn't help it.

She was staring at her sleeping bag as she said this, and Jared studied her bowed head before breaking into a deep laugh. Startled, Sydney glanced up. Jared dropped down beside her and hugged her with one arm around her shoulders. "Don't ever scare me like that again, Sydney. I mean it."

She leaned into him, savoring the feel of his reassuring strength. "I'll try not to, but you never know with me."

They laughed together as relief mingled with the satisfaction of being home together again. "So, how were Mom and Dad?" she asked. They laughed again at the absurdity of life going on despite everything, and this time she was rewarded with a good punch in the arm.

Chapter Ten

Natural optimism had returned after a good night's sleep, and Sydney went to work shoveling snow away from the barn doors with a renewed vigor. The sky was tinted a pale winter's blue without a cloud in sight, making the glare from the glittering snow hard on the eyes. Even with sunglasses, Sydney had to stop occasionally to wipe the moisture off her eyelids.

Her world seemed to have righted itself with the return of her eldest brother. She still wasn't sure she'd ever see Mark again, but in the light of day things didn't seem quite as bad as they had. Being left alone the day before had made her world a bleaker place, but she realized now that she hadn't given Mark even the slightest chance.

She remembered what a mess Paul's life had been when he was first establishing his relationship with Shannon. He'd alternated between being confident and panic-stricken, and for months he'd been downright spacey. It wasn't until he had gotten his ring on Shannon's finger that he'd settled down to his usual dependable self.

Recognizing that she was in that panic-stricken stage helped her somewhat. Nothing was certain where Mark was concerned, but there wasn't much she could do about it since she was snowed in without power or a telephone. Getting power restored this far from town was last on the list of priorities for the power company, and she knew they probably couldn't get to all the downed lines yet. Most of the side roads would be blocked for several days as the road crews concentrated on the main arteries of travel.

Being cut off from civilization didn't help. Her thoughts kept returning to Mark no matter how hard she tried to distract herself. She couldn't help wondering how he was. Had he even gone to the hospital to get checked out? She imagined him home sleeping in a rumpled bed with the covers strewn haphazardly around him. Her mind fixated on the image of one of his muscled legs peeking out from under the comforter. She wasn't sure if her memory was that good or if she was just making it up as she went along, but she could see every detail of that leg. . . .

The drone of a pickup engine startled her out of her meanderings, and she looked up to see Paul returning from blading the lane. A blush crept up her skin, and she was glad no one could read her thoughts.

It surprised her that Paul was back so soon. He'd been making a trail out to the highway, and she'd expected it to take him at least all morning. They needed groceries and supplies, and Paul and Shannon had planned to go to town later that afternoon.

Paul parked the truck by the barn and killed the engine. With the release of that noise, Sydney could still hear the whine of a motor. It mixed with the twang of wood splitting as Jared chopped wood by the side of the house. In confusion she looked down the trail Paul had made and saw a black vehicle slowly traversing the drifts.

"I wonder who that is," she called to Paul as she pointed toward it.

Paul followed her gaze and straightened from bending over the blade on his truck. He'd been adjusting the blade's angle but stepped away from it now to get a better look. He shrugged in answer as they stood together and watched the vehicle approach.

Jared set his axe down and joined them. "That looks like my ride from last night. Maybe they found out something about those kids who jumped your officer."

Paul raised his eyebrows and Sydney discreetly shook her head. Jared didn't know how she felt about Mark. She hadn't wanted to talk about it the night before, and they'd both been so tired that they'd gone to sleep without sharing too much news.

Jared hadn't meant anything by calling Mark "her officer," and she didn't bother to call attention to it now. Thankfully Paul followed her lead as they waited for the Explorer to stop.

When Kent stepped out, Jared moved forward with his hand outstretched. "It's good to see you." He gripped Kent's hand tightly and then let go. "Looks like you made it home all right last night."

"I'm glad to see you did too."

"Mark not with you?" Jared asked as he looked in the open driver's door.

"No. He's down at the station handling some paperwork. He had to make a formal statement about what happened to him and all."

Jared shut the car door as he nodded his head. "I forgot to ask you last night—have they found those guys?"

"Well, we know who they are, but we haven't apprehended them yet. Don't worry, we will."

Jared seemed to notice his brother and sister for the first time. Sydney had soaked in every word about Mark like a sponge, and she was happy to stand to the side and just listen. Paul stepped forward when Jared looked at them. Jared spoke up. "I forgot you don't know these two. This is my brother, Paul, and my sister, Sydney."

Kent shook hands with Paul first, giving Sydney more time to study him. She recognized him from the day before, but now that she had a closer look she was amazed at how much he looked like his son. Or rather how much Mark looked like him. He was dressed in jeans and work boots with a heavy leather jacket buttoned up to his chin. The resemblance between the two wasn't just in their faces as she noticed Mark was built just like his Dad.

"Sydney," Kent said almost on a sigh as he squeezed her hand. "I can't tell you how grateful I am for what you did."

The emotion in his dark eyes was so sincere that Sydney had to blink back tears of her own. "I don't think I did anything that any other person wouldn't have done." She shrugged with a shy gesture as Kent released her hand.

"You're wrong there," Kent said softly. "Any other person wouldn't have been tough enough or smart enough to do what you did. You can play it down with other people if you want, but not with me. Thank you. . . . Thank you very much."

Sydney blushed and jammed her hands into the pockets of her insulated coveralls. "You're welcome."

"People who live in the country are used to a different survival mode than town people," Paul put in. "I'm sure Sydney didn't think that much about what she had to do. She just did it."

"Well, that could be," Kent answered as he studied Sydney with a soft, fatherly expression. "That makes me even more thankful she was the one there."

Meeting his gaze was too difficult and Sydney looked at the ground. She'd been proud of herself and had known her family would be too, but praise from Mark's father embarrassed her. Paul had summed it up quite well, and she didn't feel she deserved that much recognition.

"Which brings me to why I came out here," Kent said after clearing his throat. "Your phone being out of service just made it more convenient since I wanted to meet you and invite you in person anyway."

Sydney looked up and met his eyes.

He smiled. "I had a conversation with the mayor this morning. He told me to tell you how impressed he is with what you've done. He also authorized me to invite you to an award ceremony."

Sydney pulled her hands out of her pockets and linked her gloved fingers together. "Award ceremony?"

Kent nodded. "Yes, that's right. It's for you.

For saving Mark's life. The mayor feels—not to mention every police officer in the state—that what you did was heroic, to say the least. The mayor wants to meet you in person and present you with a plaque of appreciation. The press will be there, of course. A positive story like this deserves more airtime than all that negative stuff they're always talking about anyway.''

Sydney didn't know what to say. She wasn't even sure how she should feel. Jared knew how he felt about it and jumped in to cover her silence. ''That's impressive. And I agree with you—they should put more positive stories on the news. There have to be plenty of good stories out there. If the media would concentrate on them more, maybe people would have more optimism about life than they do.'' He paused to take a breath. ''This sounds like a big honor for Sydney.''

''Oh, it is,'' Kent agreed. ''Another reason I drove out today was to make sure you could get to town tomorrow. The mayor wants to present you with the plaque at the courthouse tomorrow at eleven. He wants to take you to lunch after that.''

''Getting her to town will be no problem,'' Jared answered as Sydney continued to stand silently.

''What do you think, Sydney?'' Paul asked as he nudged her shoulder with his elbow.

She unclenched her fingers and rubbed her forehead. "I don't know for sure. I don't really think I deserve an award."

Kent squeezed her shoulder. "You know, there are police officers attacked every day, and a lot of the time there are citizens in the vicinity who don't lift a finger to help. If people could see you on television and hear your story, maybe they'd think they could make a difference too."

"You make me sound like a role model or something," Sydney answered with a shaky laugh.

"That's exactly what you are," Jared put in. "I know you're probably feeling guilty about being caught in a storm and you're probably even still defensive about keeping that horse. I know that's my fault. I admit I was wrong about the horse. If that crazy animal is capable of bringing you back to the barn when he can't see where he's going, then he deserves a good life. In fact I was thinking I'd personally give him a carrot every day myself.

"And I was upset about the storm because I was afraid. Mark said you would have made it back to the house easily if you hadn't stopped for him. That's not the same as stupidly getting caught in a blizzard. You do deserve an award, Sydney. An officer's life isn't something to be taken lightly."

Sydney's mouth fell open as she listened to Jared make the longest speech she had ever heard from him. She had joked with Mark that she lost a few battles with Jared but could still win the war, but she hadn't meant anything like this. And he was right—she had felt guilty for being caught in a storm, and his opinion about keeping Blaze had made her doubt herself. Sometimes she thought she was just a little too sentimental about her horses. Now to hear Jared say he was wrong freed her from the burden she'd been carrying, making her feel light as a helium balloon. For the second time she enveloped Jared in a hug. "Thanks," she whispered in his ear.

Stepping back, she faced Kent and wiped the moisture out of her eyes. "Please tell the mayor I'd be happy to accept his invitation."

All three men beamed at her response. Kent grasped her right hand in both of his. "Thank you. I'll tell him right away." Letting go of her hands, he stepped back. "I know Mark was disappointed he didn't see you last night when we brought Jared back. He'll be looking forward to seeing you tomorrow, as will I."

He shook hands with Jared and Paul and moved back toward his vehicle. He turned back before stepping inside. "Oh, and your whole family is invited too. And to lunch afterward. I hope you can make it."

"We wouldn't miss it for the world," Jared answered, patting Kent on the back to reinforce his delight.

* * *

Her brothers were excited for her, pestering her constantly about what she was going to say and just generally bothering her by bringing the honor up over and over again. Sydney hardly heard them after a while and hadn't a clue what she said to get them off her case because the only thing she could think about was Kent's last comment. He'd said that Mark would be looking forward to seeing her and that he'd been disappointed he'd missed her the night before.

She wondered if he really did. And if he did, what did it mean? Kent had left before she could think to ask him how Mark was doing. But obviously he'd checked out all right or Kent would have said something.

Anticipation for the next day was building within her like a river rising with spring runoff. It was steady and powerful and by the next morning had her so agitated she couldn't sit still. She hadn't a thought in her head about the award itself, even though she knew it was a tribute to her. No, all her anxiety was focused on seeing Mark again. What would he say? For that matter, what would she say?

She hadn't realized how lonely her life was when all she'd known were her horses and her brothers. Now that Mark had come in and shaken the very foundations of her existence, she knew she could never go back to the way things had been. The trouble was, she'd never been lonely before meeting Mark, but now that she had, her life seemed empty without him. Sleeping in Jared's room with only Jared in the bed above her was not the same.

However, missing Mark didn't alter the fact that there were a lot of problems keeping them apart. For one thing, even if Mark was willing to enter into a relationship with her, would he be happy living so far from town? There would be times when he couldn't even get to the highway. Like now, for instance. A man who had lived in town all his life might not care for the isolation of living on a ranch. And she knew she could never live in town herself. Being right next to the horses was everything to her.

The questions were circling in her mind like a whirling tornado until she could hardly think straight. Her family had herded her into Paul's king cab four-wheel drive for the trip to the court-house, but she hardly remembered leaving home. Jared had asked her again what she was going to say when she received her plaque, but she didn't remember what she'd answered.

Paul's two-year-old son, Kolt, was chattering excitedly about this trip, bouncing up and down in his car seat. He asked so many questions that he kept his parents and his uncle busy answering them. That left Sydney free to spin away again in her thoughts and before she knew it they were at the courthouse.

Earlier that morning she'd had doubts about what to wear, but her wardrobe left a lot to be desired. It consisted mostly of jeans, T-shirts, sweatshirts, and a few good western shirts. She'd settled on a pair of red jeans made by Silverlake with a Roper shirt in black checked with red. Her black Roper boots completed the outfit.

The power had yet to come back on, forcing her to wash her hair in freezing cold water. She never used a blow-dryer anyway, letting her naturally curly hair dry by itself until it cascaded in soft curls halfway down her back. The lack of time she spent on it brought out its natural shine, making the light streaks in her soft brown hair sparkle like flecks of gold shining in an underground mine.

Sitting by the fire to dry her hair made it smell faintly of woodsmoke, but at least it was clean. Highlighting her eyes with a touch of mascara and a dark eye shadow to emphasize her coloring completed her efforts to make herself look good for Mark.

Paul and Jared were both wearing new pairs of Wrangler jeans and heavy plaid shirts. Shannon looked the best of all in a long denim skirt and a frilly blouse. Her short brown hair bobbed about her face in a loose, intentionally messy way that enhanced the beauty of her face. She was still carrying a few extra pounds from childbirth, but her above-average height easily accepted the added weight. Clinging to her hand as he skipped along to keep up, Kolt was a miniature version of his dad, and Sydney briefly wondered if they all looked like the hicks from the sticks.

She shook her head to clear that thought. They were all proud of who they were and what they did for a living. If people couldn't accept that, then that was their problem.

"You okay, sis?" Jared asked as he grabbed her elbow and ushered her inside.

"What? Oh, yes, I'm fine."

"You seem awful nervous. You know you really don't have to say all that much. Even just 'thank you' would do it. There's no need to get so worked up."

Sydney almost laughed. "Don't worry, bro. I'll try not to embarrass us."

"That's not what I meant—" He broke off when he saw the twinkle in her eye. He gave her a little shove. "Don't start with me today. That award isn't going to keep me from making you scrub the house from top to bottom when we get home."

Sydney rolled her eyes. "Oh yeah? You and whose army?"

Paul had navigated them to the correct room and opened the door before Jared could retaliate. They all stood back and let her enter first, and she took a deep breath before striding in confidently.

There were cameras and reporters with microphones in their hands practicing for their on-air performance, and several police officers standing around in groups. Her eyes traveled quickly over the people she didn't know, looking for Mark. It wasn't until he broke away from a group and strode toward her that she saw him.

The bruise along his eye and cheek had already faded to a yellowish color, but it still looked sore and uncomfortable. There was more energy in his step as she watched him walk, and she did a double take at how handsome he was in his freshly pressed uniform. She thought she'd remembered what he looked like, but her senses flip-flopped anew as she drank in the sight of him.

"Wow! Is he the one, Dad?" Kolt asked as he jerked on his father's pant leg.

The little boy's admiration eased the awkwardness Mark felt as he approached Sydney and her family. Kneeling down to Kolt's height, he asked, "Am I the one, what?"

Kolt leaned closer to his father for reassurance. He pointed to Mark's cheek. "You got an owie. Does it hurt?" Before Mark could answer, Kolt went on, "Aunt Sydney saved you. She's getting a . . . a . . ." He fought for the word as he nodded his head up and down.

Paul looked down. "A plaque, son?"

Kolt shook his head, frustrated with the loss of the word he wanted.

"An award?" Mark answered.

With a happy smile, Kolt nodded again. "Yeah. A award. What's that?" Innocently oblivious to his poor sentence structure, Kolt basked in all the attention he was receiving.

Mark didn't realize that Kolt had already asked that question a thousand times that morning. "It's something you get when you do something really brave, like your Aunt Sydney did." Kolt nodded happily again and Mark stood up.

All doubts in Sydney's mind had fled while she'd watched Mark talk to her nephew. His face was freshly shaven, and she caught a gentle hint of a tangy aftershave that made her stomach tighten in response. His dark hair was soft and wavy, and from her view above him she noticed the strong curve of muscle in his neck and down his shoulder. She wasn't prepared for the shock of meeting his eyes when he stood up. A shiver of electricity ran through her, and she practically jumped.

Mark had taken in every detail about her as he'd crossed the floor. He hadn't missed the softness of her hair or how tiny she looked in those red jeans. He wanted to crush her to him in a fierce hug, but he forced himself to stand back. "Hi, Angel. Glad you could make it."

Sydney felt Jared jump in surprise. She lifted her chin higher and smiled. "Hi, Mark." Ignoring everyone else, she stepped forward and lifted her arms around his neck. After a slight hesitation he gripped her hard in response.

He felt so solid and secure, making her close her eyes to shut out the rest of the world. He held her a moment longer than socially acceptable, but once released she stepped back with a glowing smile. All doubts fled as her eyes roamed over his face. "You're looking a little better. How do you feel?"

Mark forgot where they were as he gazed down at her. There was a glow in her eyes and a fresh sparkle about her that he hadn't seen before. He'd thought her beautiful before, but now she was out of this world. "I feel a lot better," he managed to say. His tongue felt tied in knots, and he would have been happy to just stand and stare at her for hours.

They were gazing at each other with an unmistakable look, and Jared frowned as he watched. What exactly had gone on in his bedroom during that storm? "You do look better rested today," Jared said, a trifle too loudly, to break their fascination with each other.

Mark turned toward him, but it took a second for his eyes to clear. The suspicious look in Jared's eyes made him stand taller as he realized he'd been too obvious. "I do feel better today, thank you. Dad told me yesterday that you made it home okay in the dark the other night." He held out his hand to shake Jared's.

That his father had gone out to the ranch without him was a still a sore point with Mark. He'd thought about Sydney all day and would have loved to talk to her, but he hadn't been able to come up with a good excuse for going back out there. Most of the daylight hours he'd spent at the station anyway. Jared's grip was so strong that it brought his mind back to the present.

"He said the same about you," Jared answered.

Tension had sprung up out of nowhere, and Sydney breathed a sigh of relief when Kent appeared at her side. He hugged her briefly and then stepped back with his hands still resting lightly on her shoulders. There was such a look of unjudgmental acceptance in his eyes that she felt a rush of fondness for him wash over her in response.

"I'm glad you could make it." He looked around and took in Paul's family.

A flush spread over Sydney's face as she realized she'd left Shannon standing unintroduced all this time. The tension eased as Shannon's natural friendliness took over. Sydney had no more time to feel awkward as the reporters circled in like hovering vultures, spewing questions at her faster than she could think.

Some inner strength asserted itself in her as she calmly answered as best she could. By the time she began to feel closed in and claustrophobic, the mayor's aide broke it up and led her over to meet the mayor. Before she knew what was going on, the mayor was making a speech and handing her a plaque that had been inscribed with her name and a few short words of appreciation from the city of Fort Collins.

Things were happening so fast, she didn't have a chance to get nervous as she said a few words thanking him for the award and stating that she was glad she'd been able to help. The media seemed as satisfied with that as if they'd just killed and eaten their prey, and Sydney and her family were ushered out and given directions to the restaurant where they'd be dining.

She hadn't been given a chance to talk to Mark again and hadn't even seen him as they'd hurried back to Paul's pickup. She looked out the window for him as Paul pulled into traffic.

"You handled that well, Sydney," Shannon said, placing her hand lightly on her arm to get her attention.

Sydney turned toward her. "Oh, thanks. It went so fast, I don't even remember what I said."

"All the right things," Shannon assured her as she squeezed her arm.

Silence fell for a brief moment and again tension

built in the atmosphere. Kolt began to babble about all he'd seen, and Sydney sat back with a sigh of relief. Maybe her nephew would save her from the inquisition she could feel was coming.

"I thought you handled that well too, Sydney," Paul said in a gesture of support. "Were you nervous?"

She hesitated but couldn't remember being nervous. "I don't think they gave me enough time to be. The mayor sure must be on a tight schedule. I'm surprised he has time for this lunch we're going to."

"I was curious about who was paying for it," Shannon put in. "I asked that aide of his just after you finished speaking."

"You did?" Sydney asked, her voice rising in surpise. "What did he say?"

"He said it was coming out of the mayor's own pocket. I imagine it's a political move of some sort. I think he's up for reelection next year."

Paul and Shannon kept the conversation going, and Sydney willingly obliged, but it just made it more obvious that Jared hadn't said a word.

Chapter Eleven

They were ushered into a private dining room and immediately seated. Mark and his father were sitting at the opposite end of the table from Sydney. Jared was on her right and Shannon, Kolt, and Paul on his right. The mayor's aides were across the table from Sydney and the mayor himself was on her left at the head of the table.

The mayor was an interesting man, not at all intimidating like she'd expected him to be. She'd seen his picture on TV many times, and his impressive height and graying hair at the temples made him seem a distinguished and out of reach type of man. But she learned he had relatives who raised horses in Wyoming and easily settled into a natural conversation with him.

167

Jared joined in a discussion about politics with the mayor's aides, and Paul and Shannon were the lucky ones getting to talk to Mark and his father. Her heart eased somewhat as she saw Paul smiling and including Mark in their conversation. He'd been supportive from the beginning, so that really didn't surprise her.

Jared's tension was unusual, and she wasn't sure what to make of it. The only thing she could think of was that he was hurt that she hadn't confided in him, but it wasn't like she'd had that much opportunity to tell him. She could feel him watching her every time she glanced down the table and met Mark's gaze.

After a while she didn't care as the looks Mark was giving her seemed to convey a message. She could tell he wanted to speak to her, and she was relieved when their meal was over and the mayor announced he had to go. He invited them all to stay as long as they wanted, and he and his aides departed as quickly as they'd come.

Jared stood up as well. "Yeah, that's probably a good idea. We've got plenty of work waiting for us at home."

Nobody argued and Sydney found herself flowing along with them on their way out the door. Anxiety rippled along her nerves as desire to stay and talk to Mark warred with her responsibility to get home as her brothers wanted. Especially since one of her brothers was doing the driving.

"It was nice meeting you all," Kent said as Paul opened the door and helped Shannon and Kolt into the backseat.

Sydney glanced at Mark, and he stepped forward and grasped her arm. "Do you have work that can't wait?" he asked softly.

She had yet to clear her training arena, but she couldn't do that until Paul was finished using the blade. Until then there really wasn't much for her to do. "No, not really," she answered, ignoring Jared, who was standing imposingly next to her.

"I'd like to talk to you. I can give you a ride home later, if that's all right?"

The sun broke out from behind a cloud, brightening the day and mirroring her own emotion. "Yes, I'd like to."

Mark looked at Jared, who was still standing next to them while Paul had already gone around and climbed in his truck. Mark's silence gave Jared a chance to speak his mind without Mark having to ask for his permission to keep his sister for a few hours.

Jared nodded in response as he seemed to reach a decision in his mind. "I figure if you can't trust a cop, who can you trust?"

Kent was still standing by silently waiting, and he'd noticed the looks Jared had been giving Mark and Sydney. He didn't care for the implied message in Jared's words and spoke up. "I imagine there are as many rotten apples in the police force as there are in just about any job.'' His tone was mild, but it still grabbed Jared's attention.

Jared met his gaze, but Kent didn't look away. After a moment he answered, ''I imagine you're right. I don't smell any worms right this second, though.''

Sydney sucked in an audible breath. Her brother was taking this protection thing way too far, and she was about to let him have it when Kent burst out laughing. Mark joined in while Jared grinned. Sydney didn't think it was particularly funny and opened her mouth to say so.

Mark forestalled her. ''Come on, Angel.'' He grasped her elbow and guided her toward his red Jeep Cherokee parked a few cars behind Paul's pickup.

Sydney looked back, still wanting to put Jared in his place, but her brother was shaking hands with Kent and stepping into the truck without once glancing her way again. Paul pulled away by the time she was seated in Mark's Jeep, and as soon as Mark slid in the driver's seat she forgot all about her brother.

Here she was alone with Mark again. She hadn't expected it to happen, and now that it had she couldn't think of a thing to say. She wanted to ask him what he'd been doing since she'd seen him last and just generally soak up his presence, but instead she twisted her fingers together and looked out the front window.

Perhaps a woman more used to relationships with men would have been able to think of something to say, but Sydney couldn't. In her heart she wanted to tell him how she felt, but she couldn't get past the thought that he didn't feel the same. She didn't want to embarrass him or herself by speaking out of turn.

The silence thickened as Mark watched her look straight ahead. He couldn't help but think she was still angry with her eldest brother. "You know, Jared didn't mean anything by that. It's been his job to look out for you for most of your life now; you can't expect him to forget that overnight."

Sydney glanced toward him and let her eyes wander over his face, memorizing every detail. Talking about her brother was the last thing she wanted to do, but she still couldn't think of a coherent sentence. Instead she let her eyes speak for her as she practically devoured him with her gaze. The raw hunger she felt leaped within her like a caged lion, and she couldn't have disguised that feeling if she'd tried.

The jagged force of desire in her eyes hit him in a wave, and his stomach clenched in reaction. "Sydney." All the suppressed emotion in him broke free as he spoke her name, and he reached across the seat to pull her toward him. She floated into his arms like the angel he thought her, and he forgot about everything else as his lips found hers again.

The rapid tattoo of his heart next to her breast and the soft clench of his hair in her fist were the only things grounding her in reality as she gave herself up to him. She had indulged herself with a few romance novels in the dead of winter, but she had never really believed that such abandon was really possible.

The frantic need to be closer fueled them both to a higher plane, until Mark gathered together the last of his control and eased himself back from the edge. ''Sydney.'' This time the word sounded harsh and gravelly deep in his throat as he fought to control his breathing. He smoothed her hair back from her face and rested his forehead on hers.

His breath mingling with hers was intoxicating as she inhaled the clean masculine scent of him. She was panting as if she'd just chased down a herd of wild horses, and she still couldn't think of a thing to say. She half-expected words to ruin the heaven she had found in his arms, and she was more comfortable remaining silent.

The last bit of control he had managed to find was rapidly slipping away as he continued to hold her so close. Having her with him was too important to blow it now, and he forced himself to lean back against the door while holding her steady with his hands on her shoulders.

The break in contact startled her and her eyes flew to his.

"We need to talk, Sydney."

His breathing was still every bit as ragged as hers, but the fact that he had found the control to sit back spurred her to do the same. Fear sent out tentacles along her every nerve ending, and she twisted her fingers together as she eased back in her seat. "Okay." Her voice was only a whisper as she agreed with him.

She had pulled away from his hands, and now he ran them through his hair in agitation. "Have you ever thought of what a police officer's life is like?"

Sydney frowned as she tried to follow where he was going. This was the last thing she'd expected him to say. "Um . . . I'm not sure what you mean. I mean, I guess I told you once how much I admire what you do. I know I couldn't face the violence, stupidity, and disrespect that you have to. I'm glad that people like you can, though. I mean, we need police." She shrugged as she couldn't think of anything else to say.

Mark closed his eyes and leaned his head back against the side window as his deepest fear became reality. She'd just said she couldn't face it, but he wasn't prepared for the pain that descended over him like a dark cloud.

"Why are you looking like that?" What had she said?

Mark opened his eyes and sat forward. He knew he should start the Jeep and take her home but couldn't find the motivation to do it.

"Wait a minute." Her voice came out strong and sharp this time. "What did you mean by that question?"

"Never mind. You answered it." He still wasn't looking at her and his voice was almost lifeless.

Sydney reached over and tore the keys out of the ignition. "Uh-uh. We're not going anywhere until you answer me." The windows had fogged, sealing them into their own private world, giving her the freedom to press the issue.

Mark turned a steady gaze on her. "You said you couldn't face it. What more is there to say?"

Sydney frowned. "Why? Were you expecting me to join the force or something?"

Mark sighed and rubbed his eyes.

"Well?" Frustration had given her an energy that wasn't going to be denied.

"This is hardly the time to be joking around, Sydney."

She was shocked at his tone of voice. "Hold on a minute. Who said I was kidding? Would you just explain what you meant? I said I couldn't face being a police officer. So? I'm not one, so what does it matter?"

He stared at her again. "I didn't ask you if you wanted to be one."

"You didn't?" She tried hard to remember what he had asked. "You asked me if I knew what your life is like. After what you and I have just been through, you shouldn't have to ask me that. Yes, I know what your life is like. I wouldn't want to do it myself. Somehow, I don't think we're on the same wavelength here."

"No, I guess not."

He didn't say any more, and Sydney studied him harder. He was asking something more. Could he really be asking what she thought he was? What if he wasn't? Something inside her wanted to wipe the pain off his face so badly that she forgot about the consequences. For her there really was no choice.

The thought of all the nights she might be worrying about him out on the streets couldn't even compare to the pain of not having him at all. She knew she was strong enough to handle it, even if he doubted her. "If you're asking me what I think about living with a police officer, now that's different. I know you have weird hours and what you do is dangerous. I'm sure I'd worry if I was married to a cop, but if I loved someone it wouldn't matter.

"Come to think of it—it would take a strong man to marry me too. I travel quite a bit, and I get obsessed with my horses, and I suppose some people would think what I do is dangerous too. I like to think of myself as being strong enough to handle just about anything, but I'm not sure there's a man out there strong enough to handle me.'' She paused to take a breath. ''But that's probably not what you meant anyway, is it?'' She'd gotten his attention, and now he was staring at her with something like hope in his eyes. She held her breath as she waited.

Still feeling his way around the subject, he asked, ''Do you think you could ever fall in love with a cop?''

She shrugged. ''To tell you the truth, I think I'd fall in love with the man, and what he did for a living really wouldn't matter that much. I really don't spend that much of my time worrying. I'm more the type that thinks she's strong enough to handle whatever comes her way.'' There. She'd underscored her ability enough times that to make it any clearer she'd have to hit him over the head with it.

There was still a trace of doubt in his expression and fear gripped her again. Maybe she'd overdone it. He was probably thinking she was too hard-headed and opinionated to mess with. That thought made her cringe, and she adopted a false cheer as she asked, ''So, while we're in this philosophical discussion—what do you think of living in the country?''

He'd been groping for a way to ask her how she

felt about him, and he practically sighed in relief when she gave him a respite. "My father and I take off a couple days every summer to go camping. That's really the only time I've ever been in the country. I think it's peaceful and relaxing, and it's nice to get away from all the people. I felt the same about your house."

"Why do you live in town then?" She knew she was circling around the issue, but the conversation seemed to be working its way closer to the center.

"I guess I never thought about it. Places in the country are expensive, and even though I make decent money, it wouldn't be enough on my own. I guess I've always held out that option for when I get married."

She nodded and looked away. Without coming right out and saying she loved him, she couldn't think of any more questions around the issue.

Mark studied her expression and a slow smile began to spread the corners of his mouth. His father had been right. She was capable of handling his job. She'd shown him that by taking care of him the way she had. And her response to him when he'd taken her in his arms spoke volumes about the way she felt. Wading around the important stuff had eased his mind, but he could see it had just depressed her.

"Sydney?" Reaching out, he grasped her chin

and turned her toward him. "You are the most incredible woman I've ever met. Did I mention how beautiful you look?"

She shook her head. His expression said he meant it, but she was only wearing a pair of jeans, for heaven's sake.

He smiled at the doubt that crossed her face. "You look even more like the angel I thought you were when I first met you. I think that's when I first fell in love with you. Getting to know you since then has just sealed it deeper in my heart."

Her eyes widened in shock, and he smiled again. "I know that's pretty fast. I've only gotten to know you for a couple of days. I feel like I've known you for a long time, though."

Sydney's heart felt like it was going to burst. "Oh, Mark." Sliding closer she ran her fingers lightly down his cheek. He was still smiling, but there was a question in his eyes. Ignoring it for the moment, she indulged herself by kissing him. It was the first time she'd ever done that in her life, and she was shocked at the liquid pooling in her stomach that slowly spread out to the tips of her toes when he responded just as ardently as she.

It was easier this time for Mark to pull back. He still needed to hear how she felt, and he was impatient for her to put him out of his misery. Her eyes were glazed with desire, and he gave her a little shake.

Her eyes cleared to find his gaze boring a hole right through her. She smiled and actually laughed a breathy sound at her newfound power. "You know I was so attracted to you I could hardly hold my hands still to bandage your eye." Carefully she traced her finger around the bruising on his upper cheek. "At the time I thought you were suspicious of me. Like I was one of those people in that car, and I had kidnapped you or something. I kept waiting for you to try and arrest me or at least accuse me. I was so glad you didn't have a gun because I was sure you would have shot me when the lights went out."

She smiled as she noticed how hard he was listening to her. "That you could doubt me really bothered me and it took a long time for me to figure out why. I didn't know you, so why would your opinion mean anything? But the thing is, it did. It wasn't until you left that I had to admit I'd fallen in love with you. And even then I thought I'd never see you again. I never thought a big city cop would even look twice at a hick like me."

Mark pulled her against his chest and smoothed her hair. "How could you think that? I'd even wrangled you into eating dinner at my place. And I offered to get Jared because I thought I'd see you again that way. Didn't you realize that?"

Sydney shook her head, luxuriating in the rasp of his light blue shirt against her skin. "I thought you were just doing it out of a sense of responsibility. Like you had to pay me back for helping you or something.''

He clutched her tighter as he sighed. ''That wasn't it.''

She pulled back and lightly traced her finger over his bottom lip. ''I know that now.'' Following her finger with her lips, she settled into him like she was coming home for the first time in her life.

An underlying passion fueled the kiss, but it was tempered now with a newfound security that hadn't been there before. ''I love you, Angel,'' Mark almost groaned as they pulled apart yet again.

Her eyes grew serious. ''I love you too.''

''Will you marry me?''

Surprise widened her eyes. She had expected him to take things slowly, but he'd blown that idea right out of the water.

He saw the misgivings in her eyes. ''I know it's fast. You know, I thought I'd never get married. For a lot of reasons. But since meeting you, none of those reasons makes sense anymore. A timeline set up by society doesn't mean anything either.''

An overwhelming sense of joy spread over her like a sunny summer's day. ''I've never been one to worry much about what other people think,'' she admitted as she smiled again. ''But there's just one thing.''

"What?" he asked and held his breath as he waited.

"I can't live in town."

His breath whooshed out. "I'd love to live in the country. Jared might think three's a crowd, though."

Sydney laughed. "We can build our own house, like Paul did."

Mark wasn't too worried about the details. "Does that mean you're saying yes?"

"Yes."

The moist air inside the closed-in Jeep had gotten thick and heavy, but Mark was sure he'd found his own little bit of heaven.